KEY TO MURDER

By P. L. Gertner

First Printing: April 2018
Second Printing: November 2018
Third Printing/2nd Edition: March 2019
Audiobook: March 2019

Paperback ISBN–9781980717867

Visit my website at www.gertnermedia.com

Acknowledgements

Kudos to Sitra Bourne who did an outstanding job narrating the Key to Murder audiobook! Her great performance brought the characters and story to life.
Also, my thanks to Rena for her editing skills and for being my second set of eyes.

Books by P. L. Gertner

Ellie Nelson Series
Key to Murder – Book 1
Canvas for Murder – Book 2
Casting Call for Murder – Book 3
Plein Air Murder – Book 4

Caryn O'Neal Series
A Trace of Treachery – Book 1

PROLOGUE

All eyes followed Ellie Nelson as she walked toward her office. Mitchell Hanover, the Denver District Attorney, stood with arms crossed and feet spread, clearly blocking her way.

"You're fired, Nelson."

"On what grounds?"

"Insubordination, for starters."

"Insubordination? You've got to be kidding."

"No, I'm not kidding and that's just if you're lucky. Did you think it wouldn't get back to this office that you continued to pursue a case you had been ordered to close? Consider yourself lucky that I'm not charging you with tampering with evidence, at least not yet. I'm not sure what possessed you to go to the evidence locker for a key c33hain, Nelson. However, I do know that it is Stephen Lindsey's personal property and should be returned to his family. I don't think we need to put them through anything more."

That stopped Ellie. She just stared at Hanover for a moment. But, finally, she set her briefcase on the nearest desk. She opened the case, unzipped one of the pockets and pulled out a key chain that had a couple of keys and what looked like a rifle bullet. A "bullet key chain" had been listed in the victim's personal effects. Novelty flash drives were all the rage and Ellie had recalled seeing the bullet version the last time she was at the office supply store. She'd played a hunch and had been successful in getting the detective to sign the evidence out for her. She had been right. The bullet was actually a flash drive and had gone unnoticed by everyone.

Ellie looked Hanover straight in the eyes as she placed the key chain in his outstretched hand. She kept her voice as even as she could.

"Fine, just let me get my things."

Hanover looked down at the key chain in his hand and practically spat out his next words. "I don't know what you were thinking, Nelson. This was worth risking your career?"

Ellie simply shrugged and reached to shut her briefcase. But she was immediately stopped by Hanover.

"Not a chance, Nelson. Your files belong to the Office of the District Attorney. In fact, so does that laptop."

Hanover was pointing to the laptop that was clearly visible in the bed of her briefcase. Ellie had no problem handing the key chain over to Hanover because she had copied the contents of the bullet flash drive onto her laptop the minute she had gotten home. With the laptop also taken, Ellie was now sorry that she hadn't looked at the files more closely when she'd had the chance.

The smirk of triumph on Hanover's face raised all kinds of alarms with Ellie and she didn't miss the fact that he never mentioned the flash drive. She couldn't be sure that he even knew the bullet *was* a flash drive. She could do little more than stand there and listen to Hanover as he continued in an accusatory tone.

"We intend to go through all your files with a fine-toothed comb. And if we discover there has been any wrongdoing, we *will* bring charges. Your personal items will be shipped to your home address."

As he finished his little performance, his eyes tracked over Ellie's shoulder.

"Ah, perfect timing. Here's Security, now. They'll escort you from the building."

Ellie turned to see two Denver Sheriff's Deputies approaching her with somewhat sheepish looks. Having worked in the building for six years, she had naturally gotten to know the deputies that provided the security. Whether at the x-ray machine at the building entrance, patrolling the halls or just grabbing a sandwich in the cafeteria at the same time, these were guys she often saw. She even had a harmless flirtation going with the older of the two deputies approaching her, something his wife of 28 years knew all about and jokingly encouraged. Ellie had attended their silver anniversary party. She knew the deputies were uncomfortable, so she gave them a slight nod and a smile to let them know it was all right.

"Hey, Fred. Hey, Carl," Ellie said smoothly, "Let's get this show on the road."

She gave a quick tug of her ear as she walked by Lisa Hall. Lisa was the best paralegal in the D.A.'s office as well as Ellie's best friend. Although Ellie hadn't even looked her way, she knew Lisa had gotten the signal that meant she would call her later.

Ellie fell in step in between Fred and Carl and they maintained an uncomfortable silence as they escorted her out of the office, down the elevator, and into the parking garage to her car.

As she got into her car, Ellie broke the silence. "Don't worry, guys, I know you're just doing your job."

Ellie didn't waste any time. She pulled out of the garage, drove straight home, packed, and flew out of Denver. She hadn't liked the charade Hanover had just perpetrated and she needed some space between her and the District Attorney so that she could sort out the information she had seen on the flash drive and put it into context with what had just happened. Right now, she had some suspicions, but with the confiscation of the flash drive and her laptop, she had no way to prove them. She had to figure out a way to change that.

By P. L. Gertner

Part 1 – The Lake

By P. L. Gertner

CHAPTER 1

Ellie was in her family's vacation home at the Lake of the Ozarks. It was the first place Ellie had thought of when she had fled Denver.

"The Lake," as the locals called it, is a resort community nestled in the heart of Missouri about equidistant between Kansas City and St. Louis, the two major cities at either edge of the state. The area offers world-class boating, golf, shopping, fishing, and other recreational activities, along with a wide variety of lodging, restaurants, and state parks-- something for everyone and everything.

As with many remote spots, people flocked to the area to get away from the hustle and bustle of the big city. The rustic nature of the area was considered "quaint" and anybody who was anybody had a "place at The Lake." Families fled to The Lake on weekends and in the summer to fish, swim, water ski and just generally laze around.

The Nelson family had had a house at The Lake for over 30 years. But it had been a while since Ellie had been there. The last time had been for a family reunion on her mother's side about six years ago. Although she had never been to The Lake when her folks weren't there also, they had given her a key right before she had moved to Denver. They had told her that the house belonged to her as much as to them and she could use it any time she wanted.

It was Sunday morning and Ellie Nelson sat at the dining room table sipping her second cup of coffee and gazing out the big bay window at a winter wonderland. Just like the song said, the snow was indeed glistening. But, unlike the song, Ellie didn't hear any sleigh bells. Instead there was a sort of heavy drone, coupled with an odd scraping sound. As Ellie continued to look out the window, the sound got louder and louder until a white truck flew by on the county road that ran along the front of the house.

The truck was equipped with a huge blade on the front that was spraying snow off to the side as it barreled on by. Ellie vaguely remembered hearing the same noise a couple of times in the wee morning hours. Obviously, the road crew had been out and had been down her road several times since the storm had struck. A foot of snow the weather forecaster had said.

But, good grief, the snow plow driver must be a maniac. He had to have been going 50 miles per hour. While that might be a good sign, meaning that the roads had been cleared well enough to achieve that kind of speed, it was just plain reckless in this area, regardless of the road conditions.

Most people took the wildlife and the joggers into consideration when they drove the narrow, two-lane county road that twisted, turned and went up and down, following the contours of the surrounding terrain. Obviously, the snow plow driver was not one of those people. She hated to think of someone or something being in the path of that idiot with the snow plow.

There were people who walked or jogged each morning along the road, including Ellie. One of the first things she had done when she got to The Lake was to hit the outlet mall to get something comfortable to run in. Her schedule had been so demanding lately that she hadn't run in months. Not only had the lack of exercise contributed to her stress level, it had also contributed an inch to her waistline. She was really enjoying getting back into the routine of running 3 miles each morning.

At the outlet mall, Ellie had purchased a couple of pairs of black sweat pants and sweat shirts and a bright yellow, hooded jacket. Ellie figured the jacket would not only keep out the morning chill and the dampness, but its bright color would act as a kind of reflector. She'd be hard to miss as she jogged in the early dawn hours. The road was the only flat surface and it was what she and others used as their jogging trail, stepping off the road only when there were oncoming cars.

One of the things Ellie liked best about running in the early morning was the solitude. With few people and few cars out, it really gave you time to think. And that had been just what she'd done the first couple of days she had run. She'd gotten into a kind of rhythm during her runs, spending the first part sifting through the past couple of months in her mind, especially the days leading up to her being fired. She then floated possible courses of action through her mind as she made the turn and ran back to the house.

But that had all changed in the last couple of days. Another jogger had started intruding on her solitude and interrupting her thoughts. During her runs she had a nodding acquaintance with the other residents out for their daily exercise. There was an elderly couple who walked at a leisurely but steady pace, a young woman who was a power-walker and, then, there was "God's gift." Not that Ellie thought he was God's gift, but she was sure he considered himself to be God's gift to all women, possibly even God's gift to everybody. He just had that manner about him.

He was good-looking; there was no doubt about that. He looked to be in his early forties, with a tanned, handsome face and a slim physique that was characteristic of most serious runners. But the one thing Ellie could not get past was his height. Ellie knew there was nothing logical in her prejudice, but she had never been attracted to a short man. And this man, good-looking or not, did not appear to be any taller than Ellie's own five feet, five inches.

Even without the height issue, he'd immediately become an annoyance to Ellie because he had started making it a practice to catch up with her at some point, jog along beside her and try to start up a conversation. The first day it had been, "I haven't seen you around here before."

How original. She'd been saved from responding to that one, when she heard her cell phone ring.

"Excuse me," she had said, as she came to a standstill and reached into her pocket for her cell phone. She flipped off her yellow hood and brought the phone to her ear.

He couldn't stop without appearing rude. So, "God's gift" had just kept jogging in the direction Ellie had been going. Ellie smirked to herself and did an about face, turning back toward home and keeping the phone to her ear, in case he had looked back. She had actually let the call go to voice mail. The caller ID had shown her mother's cell phone number in the display. She had taken the easy way out and sent her mother a text saying she was staying at The Lake house. She'd been dodging an actual conversation with her mother for several days now. She knew she couldn't put it off much longer. But she needed to have everything settled in her own mind before she could stand the cross examination she knew would come when she finally spoke with her mother.

During yesterday's run, she hadn't been quite as lucky. The annoying jogger had come up quickly behind her and then fallen into step alongside her. He was a little winded from the spurt he'd had to make to catch up with her and his words came out in a raspy staccato. "Wow. Great. Jack. Et. I've got. One just. Like it."

Ellie's first thought was that she was going to have to burn the jacket, but she had simply given a non-committal "Uh-huh" reply and had stepped up her pace. She figured he must have gotten the message as he hadn't followed, and Ellie had jogged the rest of the way in peace.

Today, Ellie had no intention of going outside, at least not for a run. The crisp fall-like mornings the area had been enjoying had come to an abrupt end the previous night when a blizzard literally came in out of nowhere. The howling winds that had accompanied the winter storm had kept Ellie awake a good part of the night and she had ended up sleeping in late this morning. That was okay because she wasn't one of those die-hard joggers that ran in any kind of weather. And while the snowplow might have cleared the road enough to drive a car, she didn't think it would have provided the best footing for a jogger. So, she had not gone out for her usual run and on the bright side, she hadn't had to deal with "God's gift" hitting on her this morning. It looked like she'd be getting enough exercise shoveling snow.

CHAPTER 2

As Ellie spent a leisurely morning sipping coffee and reading the local paper, her thoughts had slipped back to Denver and she had started mulling over the reason she was hiding out in the middle of Missouri. Okay, maybe hiding out was too dramatic, but she was definitely "holed up" until she could figure out what she was going to do about her problem.

She had left Denver in a hurry, packing only a carry-on with essentials. Underwear, makeup, cell phone. She'd used her cell phone to call a cab and then to make airline reservations as she rode out to the airport. The first flight from Denver to Missouri took her into St. Louis. That suited Ellie fine. Her family lived in Kansas City and she hadn't wanted to talk with them right then. Besides, she didn't know yet what she would tell them. She wasn't sure herself what was happening.

All she knew was her latest case had been shut down by Denver District Attorney, Mitchell B. Hanover. The D.A. was planning on a bid for the governor's office in two years' time and he had become very conscious of each case and what it could do to help or hinder his chances. She had been working on a suspicious death case involving a Denver V.I.P. named Stephen Lindsey.

Their investigator had worked with the Denver detective assigned to the case and although there were some irregularities, a suspect had confessed to the murder. So, there had been nothing to prosecute. Still, something was just not right in Ellie's opinion and she had put off scheduling the sentencing and closing out the case. She had looked again at all the notes from the investigation and there were a couple of items she wanted to pursue.

However, Hanover had refused to even listen to her reasoning for keeping the case open. Lindsey had been a big deal in the community and Hanover just wanted the sentencing finalized so he could take credit. He added that if she had a problem, he would just assign the sentencing to one of the other deputy D.A.s.

But Ellie had been stubborn. She hadn't listened to Hanover. She'd gone right from her meeting with Hanover to the Denver Police Headquarters for District 1 and signed out a key chain that had belonged to the murdered lawyer.

Ellie had walked into the D. A. offices the following day and had been immediately confronted by Hanover. She figured someone at the Denver P.D. must have seen her and said something that got back to Hanover.

Ellie's thoughts were interrupted when the telephone on the kitchen wall rang. She glanced at the caller ID and decided she'd better answer. "Hi, Mom," she said, as she picked up the phone.

"Eleanor," her mother replied in her usual, formal manner, always using Ellie's full name, "How did you know it was me?"

"Caller ID, Mom."

"Well, it could have been your father."

"Oh, right, and when was the last time Dad actually made a call himself?"

"Be that as it may, Eleanor, you should answer the phone properly."

"Yes, Mom, was there a reason you called?" A hint of irritation slipped into Ellie's voice. She didn't need one of her mother's lectures today.

"You needn't get that tone in your voice, Eleanor. I was just calling to see if you were doing okay. We heard a weather report that said The Lake really got hit hard and that some homes were without power."

"I'm fine, Mom, and so is the house. We might have lost power for a bit last night because the digital clock was flashing when I got up. But there's no problem now. We did get a lot of snow, but the snow plow's been down the road several times. In fact, I was just thinking about clearing off the driveway enough to get the Jeep out."

"Well, there's a shovel out in the garage. Oh, and an old snow-blower, although I'm not sure there's any gasoline for it. Your father generally doesn't like to leave things like that in the garage once we've left the house for the summer. If we'd known you were going to want to stay at the..."

"No problem, Mom," Ellie interrupted. Now was not the time to go into the reason she had suddenly left Denver and was staying at the family's house at

The Lake. She'd texted it was just a vacation. But the fact was, Ellie wasn't sure when she'd be going back to Denver. She certainly didn't have a job to go back to and her house and car and other things would all be waiting for her once she'd made up her mind about what she was going to do. But it'd been over a week now and her mom was starting to ask questions. Ellie had never taken off more than a couple of days in a row in the six years she'd been working in the Denver D.A.'s office. And now that Ellie was going into her second week of "vacation," she knew she was going to have to bring her mom and dad up to date, but Ellie wasn't quite ready.

Ellie snapped out of her daydream as she realized her mother was saying something to her about the mailman.

"Sorry, Mom, I dropped the phone there for a second. What about the mailman?"

"Not the mail *man*, Eleanor, the mail *box*. While you're out there shoveling snow, you'd better see if the mail box is still on the post."

All the mail boxes at The Lake were placed along the edge of the road so that the local mail carrier could just drive up and put the mail in the box without leaving the car. With the way the roads wove in and out of The Lake's shoreline and the fact that some of the areas were still very much undeveloped, houses could be few and far between. So, the roadside mailboxes were the only practical way for the carriers to cover the territory they needed to each day.

Ellie's mom had gone on to explain that the snow plow drivers were notorious for clipping the mail boxes with the huge blade on the front of their truck as they cleared the road. According to the homeowner's association, the face of the mailbox was supposed to be set back ten feet from the edge of the pavement. Most of the mailbox posts had been put in long before the covenant was ever outlined and were much closer to the road. That allowed the homeowner's association and the road maintenance company to deny responsibility for any damages. It also resulted in the residents trying various ways to protect their mailboxes.

On her morning runs and her shopping trips using the Jeep her dad kept at The Lake, Ellie had noticed the wide assortment of mailboxes in various shapes, sizes, colors, and materials. Some were in much better condition than others. Several mailboxes were dented, with posts tilting to the side. Obviously, they had been previous victims of the snow plow's blade, but had been lucky enough to avoid total annihilation. There were two or three new mailboxes made of heavy-duty green plastic that had an attached sleeve encasing the entire post. Those looked like they could withstand a pretty good attack. One mailbox and post were made of metal and were painted a hideously bright orange. Another had six, round, red reflectors attached up the wood post and reflector strips lining the sides of the mailbox itself. There were even a couple mailboxes that looked like they were attached to the supporting posts with rope or bungee cords. It was pretty amusing really and Ellie could almost guess the personalities of the people inside the house that belonged to each mailbox by the way they had tried to deal with this annual occurrence.

Ellie's mom was still talking and said the family's old metal mailbox had been replaced last year after it had been rendered completely useless when it had been knocked off its post. It had been lying about ten feet from the post and was mangled so badly that the door wouldn't close. The property management company the family used to look after the house in their absence had noticed the damage and had attached a new, black plastic mailbox to the wooden post.

Before Ellie could get off the phone with her mother, she had had to assure her she would check on the mailbox and would call the property management company if she needed any help. "I'll call you on my cell phone when I get outside and let you know what's going on."

Luckily for Ellie, she and her mom were the same size, even wore the same size shoe. Since Ellie had left Denver in a hurry, she had quickly crammed everything she could into her carry-on bag while waiting for the taxi that would take her to the airport. She hadn't worried that much about what she was packing because she knew her mother had tons of clothes in storage at The Lake house.

Ellie headed straight for her mother's walk-in closet in the master suite and eyed the rows of shoe boxes stacked on the shelves above the clothes racks. Her mother was very organized, and all the boxes were labeled. Ellie scanned over "red sling backs," "black penny loafers," "navy boat shoes," and a host of others until she came to one that read "brown winter boots."

The boots were perfect for what Ellie was about to do. As with most things her mother bought, they were stylish but quite functional. According to the markings on the box, these were "waterproof, shearling-insulated Ulu boots, inspired by the resilient people of the Arctic." Ellie slipped her stockinged feet into the right boot and immediately fell in love. The shearling lining seemed to mold around and cushion her foot at the same time. She pulled the boot tops up over her jeans and used the well-placed leather tabs and laces to close up the boot, which hit her just below the knee. She quickly put on the left boot and went to look at herself in the full-length mirror just outside the closet. Wow! She was either going to have to see if her mother would part with these or she was going to have to find out where she could get a pair just like them.

After one last glance at herself in the mirror, Ellie went to the closet in the foyer and pulled out her gloves and the down parka she had worn from Denver. She picked her cell phone up as she went by the dining room table and stuck it in the Velcro tabbed pocket on the parka's left sleeve. It was amazing how everything they made these days seemed to have a place for all the latest gadgets. Cell phones, iPods, Blackberrys, whatever, could be tucked away so that you could always stay connected or listen to music no matter what you were doing or where you were going.

Ellie was never without her cell phone and the pocket on the sleeve had actually been the deciding factor between the parka and another coat Ellie had been considering buying. Ellie pulled on her gloves and then headed out to the garage to look for a shovel.

The garage was her father's domain and he was just as organized as her mother. Her dad's Jeep Wrangler was in the first bay of the two-car garage. The second bay was empty and available for whatever car he and her mother drove down from Kansas City whenever they wanted to get away for a few days. Once at The Lake, the Jeep became the car of choice as it was better for the hilly terrain and to navigate some of the roads in the area that were still dirt or gravel. Around the sides and back of the garage were built-in work tables, shelves, peg boards and cabinets filled with every tool imaginable.

Ellie stepped over to the cabinet she knew contained the shovel, along with a broom, a rake, and a weed eater. She also saw the snow blower sitting over in a corner. But even if there were gasoline, she really didn't want to mess with it and hated the loud drone it made when it was powering up.

She pulled out the shovel and pushed the button that would open the automated garage door. When it had opened, Ellie got her first look at just what was in store for her. The snow was every bit as deep as they had said, and it drifted in spots to what looked more like two feet, especially at the end of the driveway where the snow plow had created a barrier between the driveway and the road. Ellie wasn't sure she was up for shoveling the whole driveway and cutting through the snow plow's bank. She decided she'd go out to check on the mailbox and get a feel for how packed the snow was.

The snow was fairly light and fluffy, and Ellie began to wonder if she could just put the Jeep in four-wheel drive and drive back and forth, packing down the snow enough to make a path out to the road.

As Ellie reached the end of the driveway, she looked off to the left toward the mailbox. But all she saw was the post sitting at an angle, no mailbox atop it. She started looking around and saw the mailbox sticking out of a snow drift about five feet on the other side of the driveway opening. "Wow, that had to have been knocked a good fifteen feet away from the post," Ellie thought to herself.

She trudged across the driveway and was bending over to pull the black box out of the drift when she also noticed something bright yellow lying in the snow. It looked like her yellow jacket.

As Ellie stepped closer, she could see it was a yellow jacket all right. But other than that, her brain wasn't initially processing the scene very well. What was her yellow jacket doing out in the snow? Why was someone else wearing it? And most importantly, why was that person lying face down in the snow? Ellie's first thought was that the crazy snow plow driver had unknowingly hit someone.

But Ellie quickly shook off the confusion as her emergency medical training kicked in. She had taken the training when it had been offered to any Denver officials that were interested. She had never had to use the training up until now, but she knew what to do. She debated for a moment about whether turning the person might cause more injury, but she needed to expose the carotid artery in the neck to check for a pulse and turn the head so the person could breathe. She decided she had to risk moving the person.

It took some doing because the body was pretty much encased by the deep snow. After Ellie got as firm a foothold as she could, she rocked the body, gently at first, and then she pulled back as hard as she could. As the body rolled over, Ellie was propelled backward into a snow drift. When she was able to get back on her feet, she brushed the snow off her boots and clothes as well as she could and then bent down once again over the body.

And it was definitely a body. Ellie could no longer think of it as a person even though she recognized the face staring back at her with dull, blank eyes. The person was gone and only a lifeless body remained. And that body had once belonged to none other than "God's gift." The man had annoyed Ellie, but he obviously had annoyed someone else a whole lot more. The tinge of blood in the snow and the bullet hole in the yellow jacket certainly proved that.

One look at the lifeless eyes and Ellie knew there was no reason to check for a pulse. That was just as well, because she would have had to untie the cord that held the bright yellow hood securely on his head. Investigators tended to get a little testy when anyone disturbed a crime scene. And Ellie figured she had already disturbed it enough with all the snow she had flung around trying to roll the body over, not to mention where she had stepped and knelt beside the body. She knew whatever investigator showed up was not going to be very happy with her.

CHAPTER 3

Ellie pulled her cell phone out of her parka and dialed 911. She informed the 911 dispatcher she had found the body of someone who had been shot. She followed that with the location and her name.

"A deputy will be there in about five minutes," said the dispatcher, "along with an emergency medical team."

"It's too late for the E.M.T.s," Ellie responded. "This man is dead, and this was no accident. I know the E.M.T.s are procedure, but you're going to want to call in a homicide detective and your medical examiner."

The dispatcher obviously gave little weight to her comments.

"Ma'am, just stay put until help arrives. They'll know what to do."

Ellie clicked off her cell phone. She hated being patronized. Having been a prosecuting attorney, she had been to her share of crime scenes and had handled evidence for cases too numerous to count. While you never got used to the innumerable ways the human species could find to kill someone, and it was never a pretty sight no matter what the method, Ellie did know the routine. She knew about contaminating a crime scene and what that could do to an investigation and the ultimate prosecution if the case came to trial. But she cut the dispatcher a little slack. He didn't know her from Adam, and he was following procedure.

As she waited for the promised "help" to arrive, she stood staring down at the head enclosed in the bright yellow hood. "God's gift" had been right. He did have a yellow jacket just like hers. Now Ellie was sure she was going to have to get a new jacket. No way could she put hers back on and not picture lifeless eyes staring out at her.

Ellie heard sirens in the distance and she began stepping back through her tracks in the snow to put a little distance between herself and the body. Just then her cell phone rang. Ellie looked at the caller ID and saw it was her mother. She thought about letting it go to voicemail but knew her mother would continue to call. So, she sighed and hit the button to take the call.

"Hi, Mom."

"Eleanor, you said you would call me."

"Yes, Mom, I know that, but I got a little busy. There's a problem."

"So, the mail box *did* get knocked off again?"

"Well, yes, there was that. But, there's something more serious. I…"

"Eleanor, do I hear sirens? "

The authoritative tone in her mom's voice was starting to slip, and then it disappeared altogether.

"Ellie, are you all right?"

That brought a slight smile to Ellie's face. Her mother very seldom displayed anything but the formal, straightforward manner that had gotten even stronger as she worked her way up the ladder to become one of the managing partners of a major law firm in Kansas City. The persona presented to her corporate clients was the same one Evelyn Nelson usually presented to her family and friends.

So, while on the surface Ellie and her mother's relationship seemed to be a bit stiff and even strained to a casual observer, the two women actually had a very strong bond. Their verbal sparring was actually an intricate game of "one-upmanship" that they each enjoyed, if the truth were known.

So, Ellie knew her mother was concerned when she dropped the Eleanor and called her Ellie. She didn't have time to tell her mother what had happened, but she, too, softened her tone.

"Yes, Mom, I'm fine, but I've got to go now. The Sheriff's here. I'll call and explain later. Love you, both. Bye."

Ellie wasn't really listening for a response from her mother at that point and she ended the call as she watched a Sheriff's car pull up and come to a stop on the far side of the road. She might have wished she had listened though. Because as soon as Evelyn Nelson had heard Ellie say "Sheriff," she had turned to her husband and said, "Howard, that's it, something is going on. I'm going to cancel everything I've got going next week and you'd better do the same. We're going down there."

Since Ellie's driveway hadn't been cleared, the deputy had left the patrol car in the far lane of the county road, lights still flashing, but the siren mercifully shut off. Out of the car stepped one of the county Sheriff's deputies. He couldn't have been more than twenty-five and looked more like fifteen. He was about 5' 10' and had a round, baby face, complete with rosy cheeks. He was carrying at least 60 extra pounds and the uniform jacket he was wearing only emphasized his bulk.

Ellie couldn't help but wonder how much help he was going to be. She was willing to give him the benefit of the doubt and smiled slightly as he started across the road toward her.

"Are you the one who called, Ma'am?"

"Yes, I'm Ellie Nelson and I'm the one who called in the dead body."

Ellie gave a slight nod in the direction of the bright yellow jacket sticking out of the snow.

The deputy followed her gaze and started walking toward the body.

"Wait! You might want to wait for your crime scene investigator."

But the deputy either wasn't listening or figured he wasn't going to take any suggestions from a civilian. He walked over to the body and looked down at the face. Ellie watched as his face registered shock, and then went green.

Ellie could see the deputy fighting for control and knew what was coming. "Away from the body," she yelled.

The deputy surprised Ellie. He managed to take a deep breath, and while he still looked a bit pale, he hadn't added anything further to the crime scene. He pointed at Ellie and said, "Don't you move, Ma'am," and then walked back across the road to his car, with his head tilted slightly to the side as he talked into the radio on his shoulder.

From his reaction, Ellie guessed the deputy had known "God's gift." That was still how Ellie thought of him, because she had never given the guy a chance to tell her his name. But she figured she'd be learning soon enough.

Ellie hadn't planned on moving and continued to wait as more emergency vehicles started to pull in behind the deputy's car. First another Sheriff's car, then the fire rescue ambulance and an unmarked car Ellie figured might belong to the medical examiner.

The deputy had apparently put out the word that this wasn't a prank call and it wasn't anything ordinary. The vehicles strung along the road, lights flashing, blocking the driveways of the two houses across the road from the Nelson's house. She could see the neighbors had come out of their houses and were trying to see what was going on.

The man in the second Sheriff's car seemed to be the one in charge, and from the way the deputy was deferring to him, Ellie assumed the newcomer was either a very senior deputy or the Sheriff, himself. He spoke with the deputy for a few minutes, glancing occasionally over toward the body and toward Ellie, following the gestures that seemed to punctuate whatever the deputy was telling him. He gave the deputy a little pat on the back and gestured toward the neighbors. Probably sending him off to gather witness statements and giving him an 'atta boy' for keeping his cool and not losing his breakfast.

Ellie thought that showed the signs of a good cop who cared about his men. She watched as he then motioned to the man who had pulled up in the unmarked car, and together, they walked over to the body.

They stopped just in front of the body. The Sheriff and the civilian looked down at the body and exchanged a look. It was obvious that they, too, recognized the unfortunate person lying dead by Ellie's driveway. The Sheriff then nodded to the civilian who took out a camera from the backpack he had slung across his shoulder. The Sheriff left the civilian to what he was doing and continued on toward where Ellie stood.

He took it slow and chose his path carefully as he came over to Ellie.

"I'm Sheriff Duncan. You want to tell me who you are and what happened here?"

"I'm Eleanor Nelson. Ellie. This is my folks' place. I've been vacationing here for the past week."

Ellie paused and waited for the Sheriff to respond, but he said nothing. So, she went on to explain that she had noticed the bright yellow jacket sticking out of the snow when she had come out to shovel the driveway and to check to see if the mailbox had been knocked off its post. She pointed to where the black mailbox still lay, forgotten in all the commotion.

"I'm sorry about messing up your crime scene, but I was trying to help the person and thought it was probably just an accident, until I saw the bullet hole."

"You a fan of CSI are you, Ms. Nelson?"

"What? Oh, no, sorry. I am, or I was, a Denver Deputy District Attorney."

Other than an almost imperceptible nod, the Sheriff continued as if they hadn't even had the exchange.

"How did you know Doug Withers?"

"Doug Withers? Is that his name? Sorry, I didn't even know that. I'd only seen him the last couple of mornings when I was out running."

"Any conversation?"

Ellie didn't see the need to tell the Sheriff the guy had been trying to hit on her. "Just the casual stuff. Hi. Nice morning."

"Were you running with Mr. Wither's this morning?"

"I didn't run *with* Mr. Withers. I saw him when I was running. But I didn't run today at all. I'm not a fanatical jogger, which Mr. Withers obviously is, er, was. I like a dry path."

The Sheriff continued asking questions and Ellie had told him she usually jogged just after dawn. She told him the two times she had seen Doug Withers and it was about halfway through her 3-mile run and she could never recall seeing him near her house.

Ellie had just gone through her story for a second time when the Sheriff's attention was drawn back to the road as a horn honked a bit in the distance. He could see traffic was starting to back up on the county road, in both directions. Normally, there wasn't a lot of traffic on the road. It was the only road in or out of the neighborhood and it ended in a cul de sac about two blocks further down. But it was eleven a.m. on a Sunday morning and there were folks coming and going from church, brunch, shopping, or whatever else they wanted to do on a Sunday. Two more patrol cars came around the line of cars and pulled to a stop one behind the other facing down the wrong side of the road.

Ellie could see that the Sheriff's interest in her was fading and that he was ready to get back to the crime scene, give instructions to his deputies and deal with the locals who were obviously getting impatient with the road being blocked. Sure enough, the Sheriff turned back to her and pretty much dismissed her.

"I think I've got the picture. There may be some questions for you later. But for now, why don't you go on back in your house. I'll send one of my deputies in a bit to take down your statement."

Ellie nodded, turned and walked back toward the house. She was glad to leave all the commotion behind her as she went through the garage and lowered the automatic door, shutting out the noise as well.

She realized she had been outside for over an hour and the cold had started seeping through, even with her down parka and the Ulu boots. She would have loved to go soak in the whirlpool tub to get the chill off but knew the deputy would be at her door before long. So, she decided she might as well make another pot of coffee and plant herself in front of the bay window to watch what was happening in her front yard.

CHAPTER 4

Sheriff Duncan walked back over to the body and addressed one of the county's medical examiner investigators. "Are you about done, Doc?"

"Sure am, Ken. I was just waiting for you."

The Sheriff nodded. "Good, we can clear some of this out of here."

He spoke to one of the two newly arrived deputies walking toward them. "Smith, let's get that ambulance down here so Doc can have 'em transport the body. Then let's get this area marked off and start moving the traffic."

The Sheriff then turned to the M.E. investigator and asked, "What have you got, Doc?"

"Hard to say with the cold temperature and the snow keeping the body cool," the doctor replied. "But I'd say he's only been dead three or four hours."

"The lady said she'd seen him jogging in the early mornings. So, that would fit if he was out here this morning. I never understood joggers, especially in this weather."

The doctor didn't respond. He'd known Ken Duncan for years and he knew he was just making an idle comment while his mind processed what it was seeing.

"Looks like a small caliber and not from close up. Is that how you see it, Doc?"

"I'm afraid so, Ken. Might see the bullet once we move the body if it isn't still lodged inside. Either way, I don't think you're going to find much else right here. From the way the body fell, I'm guessing the shot came from somewhere up that hill. Maybe somebody positioned up at the end of that little road that shoots off up there. They'd have a clear shot to this area."

"It looks like a pretty clean shot. So, I'm thinking we're not going to find any other stray bullets. Probably wouldn't find them in this snow even if there were some," the Sheriff grumbled. "Whoever did this was a good shot and we've got a lot of those in these parts. I'll send Smith up the road a bit to see if he can find where the shooter might have been."

The two men were interrupted as the fire rescue ambulance pulled up alongside. The deputies had gotten the ambulance through and turned around and had started directing the other traffic down the open lane. Human nature being what it is, the same people who had been impatient to get down the road, now drove along at a snail's pace, craning their necks as they came up even with the scene trying to get a look at what was happening.

The deputy was emphatically motioning the cars to come through. But it didn't seem to affect the driver's any, they'd waited for a good amount of time and now they wanted to see the reason why. The deputy was already exasperated, when a big, black Chevy Suburban pulled up, came to a complete stop and a man jumped out making a beeline toward where a couple of E.M.T.s were lifting the body into a body bag.

"Hey," shouted the deputy, "you can't..."

"Stop right there," the Sheriff said, although he needn't have bothered. The man's sense of urgency had visibly diminished after he got a look at Doug Withers body. He had turned, faced the Sheriff and flipped open a case, showing his identification.

"Special Agent Cordell Sinclair, F.B.I. What happened here?"

The Sheriff didn't look happy. "You all go on and finish up," he called to the E.M.T.s as he stepped up to the Special Agent.

"Agent Sinclair, was it? How about letting me see that ID again and you explaining why the F.B.I. might be interested in this incident."

"It's *Special* Agent Sinclair," the F.B.I. agent responded as he once again showed his F.B.I. credentials to the Sheriff. "I'm here to interview a Ms. Nelson staying at this address. Naturally, when I saw all the emergency equipment, I was concerned that Ms. Nelson might have been injured. I can see that's not the case. Sorry, to have overacted. What happened?"

The Sheriff didn't answer for a moment. He knew he wasn't getting the full story and the friendly tone the agent was now displaying was a complete 180 from the hard as nails look he had about him when he'd first jumped out of his SUV. The Sheriff took a more careful look at the F.B.I. ID and then stared hard into the agent's eyes. He was pretty good at sizing people up and this one was definitely the type to keep things close to the vest. The Sheriff was usually that type of man himself. But he decided there was nothing to be gained here playing the usual local versus federal jurisdiction games.

"Well, *Special* Agent Cordell W. Sinclair," the Sheriff said, emphasizing the "Special" and using the agent's full name shown on the ID, all the while matching the same casual tone and facial expression. "How about you move that SUV around on this side of the road behind our other vehicles, so we can get traffic moving. Then, come on back here and I'll fill you in on what we've got. After that, we can decide if this is just one big coincidence or if you need to give me a little more insight as to what you're really doing here."

Special Agent Sinclair, Cord to his friends, gave a brief nod to the Sheriff and went back to his car. He was smiling to himself as he drove down the road looking for a spot to turn around to get back to the Nelson house. The Sheriff was obviously more than competent, and although it wasn't necessarily so, Cord would have bet that he'd had some experience with a major police force somewhere before he'd landed in this area. Possibly some military background, too. The man just had a confident air about him and obviously had some intelligence behind his "good ol' boy" façade.

As the Sheriff had said, this could just be a coincidence. But Cord didn't like coincidences and he needed to know the details of what had happened. It would be better to have the Sheriff as a friend and he decided to handle things that way as he maneuvered the car and parked where the Sheriff had indicated in back of the other vehicles at the scene. He walked back in time to hear the Sheriff giving directions to one of the deputies.

"Smith, use your cell phone camera and you and Gordon walk on up the road there and see if you can find any trace of where the shooter might have been. Pay close attention up by where that road joins in. If you see anything, let me know on your radio and then start taking pictures until I can get to where you are."

As the Sheriff finished giving the instructions to the deputies, he turned toward Cord.

Cord smiled and extended his hand. "Let's start over, I'm Cord Sinclair."

The Sheriff didn't hesitate. "Ken Duncan," he said as he shook Cord's hand. "I'm the Camden County Sheriff and that's Doc Wheeler. Doc has a practice in the area and is one of the county's medical examiner investigators."

"Good to meet you," said Doc, as he, too, shook hands with Cord. "Don't take it personal, but I need to get going. Ken, I'm guessing you're going to want me to make this a priority."

"Normally, I'd say it could wait until tomorrow. I know you've got company in town but you and I both know that the proverbial excrement is going to hit the fan when word of this gets out. The more we know before then, the better it will be for all of us."

"Yeah, and that's just what I'm going to tell Martha, but she's going to go ballistic anyway. And you know she's going to take it out on both of us. So, I wouldn't be expecting any invitations to dinner any time soon. I'll call you when I'm finishing up with Withers."

The Sheriff had a half-grin on his face as he watched the Doc walk away. He turned back to Cord. "Doc's married to my sister. I love her to pieces, but she can be a difficult woman. Doc's sister and her family were down from St. Louis this weekend. She and Martha are sociable but not bosom pals, if you know what I mean. Doc's brother-in-law parks himself by the bar and drinks all his best stuff, and even Doc admits his niece and nephew are a royal pain. Martha's good manners and the fact that Doc had promised to give her a break and take them on a sightseeing trip today was all that was keeping her from telling them just what she thought of them as houseguests. It's going to be a tense day at the Wheeler household."

Cord didn't see the Sheriff as the chatty type and wondered if he was stalling or just talking while he decided on his next move. Cord got his answer when the Sheriff paused and looked directly at him. "Murder usually affects a lot of people, and this one is no different. So, let's figure out how this one affects you. Tell me again, why you're here."

Cord lied easily, looking directly at the Sheriff. "Like I said before, just a routine interview for a background investigation. Somebody up the line wants a clearance to go through in a real hurry and this is the last reference we need to check. I can't see that it has anything to do with this, but I don't like coincidences. You said it was murder?"

The Sheriff stared hard at Cord for a minute, but didn't push for any more details on why he was there. They both knew Cord wasn't telling the real reason he was here. With an almost imperceptible shrug, the Sheriff said, "Local guy. Out jogging this morning. Shot from a distance. Probably from up that hill. Clean shot right in the heart with a small caliber weapon."

"Any idea who'd want to kill the guy?"

"More like who wouldn't want to kill him. His name is Doug Withers. He's an alderman and a big shot developer in the area and likes to think he's a player. Into all the local politics. He's got a couple of projects in the works that aren't popular with a lot of the locals who don't like how fast things are changing around here. He's got a running feud with his neighbor, who doesn't believe in covenant agreements. Two lawsuits are pending on property he is trying to get rezoned and there's an alderman who has publicly threatened to kill him at the last two town meetings."

While Cord still didn't like the coincidence, he could see nothing that would tie to anything he was doing. "Well, thanks, Sheriff, I can see this isn't my business and I've taken up enough of your time. If you'll excuse me, I'll just get on my way with my interview. If you need me to move my car, let me know. Good luck."

Cord could feel the Sheriff's eyes on him as he turned his back and began walking toward the Nelson's front door.

CHAPTER 5

Ellie had watched the entire scene since Mister Tall Dark and Handsome had jumped out of his SUV. Wow, was he hot. "Hot?" Ellie had laughed at herself. She had felt like a schoolgirl for a minute as she had actually given a quick thought to calling her friend Lisa in Denver, just to describe the hunk of manhood, as Lisa liked to say, who stood outside her house. Lisa would have made her describe every detail. Six feet two, dark brown hair, a ruggedly handsome face and what she was sure was a great body. The overcoat he was wearing did nothing to disguise the image of broad shoulders and narrow hips. And the coat! Even from her distance looking out the window, the coat just screamed class and, well, money.

Ellie had been oddly disappointed when he had gotten into his SUV and driven off. She had gone into the kitchen to refill her coffee cup and told herself she was losing it. Why should it matter to her whether or not some guy she had been watching out the window had driven off? She told herself the morning's events must have affected her more than she had given them credit.

She had just about convinced herself that she was just stressed, and everything would be just fine as soon as she could finally relax in a hot bubble bath. But when she sat back down at the table with her coffee and looked out the window once again, her heart did that old cliché thing. Ellie could swear it had skipped a beat. She realized she was holding her breath and let it out slowly, telling herself to get a grip.

Mister Tall, Dark and Handsome was back. He had parked his SUV on the road in front of her house and had walked back over to the Sheriff. Ellie watched as everyone shook hands, she watched the doctor leave and then she gave an involuntary gasp as she saw the man start trudging through the snow across the lawn to her front door. This was definitely not a deputy coming to take her statement.

The doorbell rang and Ellie walked through the foyer, opened the door and looked at the man who stood before her. He was even better close up. She looked up into intense, deep brown eyes, a perfect nose and mouth, and...

With a start, Ellie realized she was staring and hadn't even said hello. Come to think of it, the man hadn't said anything either and he was now looking at her with an odd expression.

Ellie regained her composure and was the first to speak. "Can I help you?"

The man hesitated just slightly, and the odd expression was replaced by one that was all business. Just as she had seen him do with the Sheriff, he flipped open a leather case that showed his picture next to F.B.I. credentials.

"I'm Special Agent Sinclair," he said. "I need to speak with you, Miss Nelson. May I come in?"

"F.B.I.? The Sheriff said one of the deputies would be coming in to take my statement. What does a local murder have to do with the F.B.I.?"

"I'm not here in connection with whatever happened outside. I've got some questions for you about an investigation into the activities of Jack Manetti."

Now it was Ellie's turn to hesitate. She wished she could feign surprise and say she had no idea why the F.B.I. would want to talk with her about Jack Manetti. But that was simply not the case. Jack Manetti and his various activities were frequent topics in the Denver District Attorney's office, even if the discussions rarely resulted in enough information with which to build a prosecution. So, of course, Ellie would have some insights on Jack Manetti. The question was exactly which activities of Jack Manetti's were of interest to the F.B.I. And, more importantly, did they know what Ellie knew based on recent events in Denver. Ellie wasn't sure where this conversation was headed, but her curiosity was sure piqued.

"I see. Please come in. I was just about to fix myself another cup of coffee. Would you like some?"

"If it's no trouble, yes." Cord followed Ellie as she led him into the dining room and motioned him to the chair across from where she had been sitting at the dining room table.

"Well, I was just going to fix myself some French press, when you rang the doorbell. It does take a few minutes, but I can guarantee you'll like it."

Cord removed his overcoat and draped it over one of the dining room chairs, all the while watching Ellie as she walked toward the kitchen. The dining area flowed right into the kitchen and Cord could see how it would really be a good layout for entertaining. A person could be in the kitchen and still be a part of whatever was going on in the dining and living area. It also made it easy for Cord to see a half a pot of coffee sitting in an automatic coffee maker on one of the kitchen counters. It was obvious to him that Miss Nelson was delaying their discussion.

"Oh, you don't need to fix anything special. I'd be happy with what you've got made there."

Ellie did a little stutter step but recovered quickly.

"Oh, no! That's been there all morning. I should have dumped it out."

And that's just what she did, before he could make a liar out of her.

Ellie needed some time to get her thoughts together and preparing the French press coffee would buy her a little time. You had to bring the water just to the point of boiling, grind the beans, and then steep the two together in a special pot that pressed the freshly ground coffee through the hot water. The result was a rich infusion of taste and an aroma that was a delight to the senses. She busied herself getting cups out of the cupboard and setting up a serving tray with cream and sugar, while waiting for the water to near the boiling point. She could feel the F.B.I. agent watching her, but she wouldn't let herself even glance that way.

As Cord watched Ellie in the kitchen, he tried to make sense of what had happened just a few moments ago when she had first opened the door to his knock. It was like he had been struck dumb for a moment, and he could almost feel a jolt of electricity pass between them. He'd had to force himself to ignore the physical attraction he had felt and concentrate on the reason he was there.

He had seen a picture of Ellie Nelson in the file he had been given in Kansas City. The file photo hadn't done her justice. She had flaming red hair that framed a face featuring high cheekbones, liberally sprinkled with freckles. Usually that description would conjure up an image of the girl next door, but that's not the vibe Cord got from this woman.

There was an edge here, a spark of some kind that set her apart. Maybe it was intelligence or confidence. He wasn't exactly sure why, but he found her fascinating at first sight. Her blue eyes seemed to be flecked with bits of green that he was sure could shoot icy daggers at anyone who was unfortunate enough to be in her disfavor.

In the kitchen, the four-minute timer sounded, signaling the coffee had steeped for the appropriate length of time. Ellie poured coffee into two, bright orange Festival Ware mugs and placed them on the tray. Ellie placed the tray in the center of the dining room table and then sat in the seat across from Cord. She took one of the mugs and motioned for Cord to take the other.

Ellie was not shy of taking charge of any situation, but she decided that her best course of action was to wait out the Special Agent across from her and let him take the lead.

For his part, Cord reached toward the tray and added a little cream and sugar to his coffee before lifting the cup to take a sip. He could see the brief hint of uncertainty he had noticed earlier was no longer evident in Ellie Nelson's manner. The woman sitting across from him seemed sure and confident and not in the least intimidated to have an F.B.I. agent sitting across from her.

"This is terrific coffee," Cord said. "I haven't had French press for quite a while. Thanks."

Ellie smiled and gave a brief nod of her head to acknowledge the compliment, but she said nothing. She was a little surprised that the agent had been familiar with French press coffee, but as she waited for him to get to the point, her eyes had taken in the overcoat he had draped across the dining room chair next to him. She'd bet that it was cashmere. And the dark blue blazer he was wearing didn't look like it had come off the rack at Sears. So, this was not just any run of the mill agent sitting across from her. He obviously had a taste for the finer things.

Cord pulled out a small tape recorder from the inside pocket of his sport coat and set it in front of him on the table.

"As I indicated before, Miss Nelson, I'd like to ask you some questions about Jack Manetti. There is a joint investigation being conducted by the F.B.I.'s Denver and Kansas City Organized Crime Units. Jack Manetti is a primary focus of that investigation and we believe you might have some information that will aid us in our investigation. If you have no objections, I'd like to record our conversation."

"Actually, I do mind, at the moment. First, I'd like to know a little more about the investigation. Second, I'd like to know why you think I..."

A knock at the door interrupted Ellie.

"Excuse me."

Cord stood as Ellie got up and he watched as she walked around the table and crossed the foyer to the front door.

Ellie opened the door to one of the Sheriff's deputies.

"Ma'am, the Sheriff asked me to come in and take your statement."

"Certainly," Ellie said, "Come in. Special Agent Sinclair and I were having some coffee. Can I make you some?"

"No thank you, Ma'am."

The deputy followed Ellie over to the table and stopped next to where Cord was seated.

"Special Agent Sinclair, the Sheriff says he needs you to move your car out off the road. He just had the road crew clear Ms. Nelson's driveway and he said you should pull your SUV in there if it was okay with Ms. Nelson."

"That was very kind of the Sheriff. Please thank him for me when you get the chance. I have no problem if Special Agent Sinclair wants to pull his car into the driveway."

Cord picked up his tape recorder, put on his overcoat and headed toward the door. "I'll be back in just a couple of minutes."

Cord walked out the door and through the snow that still covered the walk leading from the house to the street. He glanced over to the driveway and saw the crime scene tape marking the area where the body had lain. The Sheriff and a couple of deputies could be seen farther up the road at the crest of a hill marking off another area. They had obviously found where they thought the shooter had been.

It had nothing to do with Cord, or so he thought. He got in his car and drove it into the driveway. He parked, got out, and walked quickly back to the front door. He wanted to see how Ellie Nelson handled herself during the deputy's interview. Cord stamped the snow from his feet on the mat in front of the door. He gave a quick knock on the door, turned the doorknob and stepped inside. "I'm back," he called out, removing his overcoat once again as he walked from the foyer toward the dining area.

Cord's entrance had come just as the deputy had asked Ellie how many times she and Doug Withers had jogged together. Cord could see Ellie was a bit annoyed. She glared at him as he sat back down at the far end of the table. He thought for a minute she was going to ask him to leave. But the moment passed, and she turned her glare back toward the deputy.

"I didn't say we had jogged together. As I told the Sheriff, I didn't even know the deceased's name until just a bit ago. The last couple of days, he just happened to be jogging at the same time as I was. The first morning he was jogging toward me and the second day he came up from behind me about 5 minutes into my run."

"And you said you hadn't had a conversation with him?"

"That's right."

"He said nothing at all?"

Cord watched as Ellie obviously thought about what she was going to say next. After the briefest of pauses she looked at the deputy.

"As I said, we did not have a conversation. The first day he changed direction to jog alongside me and he said something to the effect of he hadn't seen me here before. I didn't respond as my cell phone had rung and as I took the call, I turned around and walked back toward my home. I presume he continued running in the opposite direction as I didn't see him again before I got home."

"And did he say anything the second time he jogged with you...I mean the second time you saw him while you were jogging."

The deputy seemed to be trying to stifle a grin and Cord did his best to do the same. But it was obvious to both himself and the deputy that the dead guy had been trying to hit on Ellie. He looked at Ellie and saw those green flecks start to flare out from the surrounding blue in her eyes. Uh oh.

Ellie glared at both Cord and the deputy in turn. "Oh, get a grip. The guy was pathetic. Probably learned his pick-up lines from one of you. You're all cut from the same mold."

Cord had to give the deputy some credit. He didn't respond to the taunt and knew he needed to get the interview back on track. The deputy wiped the smile off his face.

"Yes, Ma'am. Uh, what else did he say to you?"

"He commented on my jacket and said he had one just like it. He..."

"Wait a minute," Cord interrupted, "He said he had a jacket like yours? What jacket? Can I see it?"

"You can have it as far as I'm concerned," quipped Ellie. "I was already thinking about trashing it when he said he had one just like it. After seeing his head inside the hood with a bullet hole smack in the middle of his chest, I was actually thinking of burning it."

Cord knew he was interfering with the deputy's interview, but he didn't much care at this point. He had a bad feeling about this.

"Miss Nelson, are you saying that the jacket the dead guy outside was wearing was just like the one you have?"

"That's exactly what I'm saying. He obviously had it on today, thinking we'd be 'twinsies'. Yuck and double yuck. Like I said, pathetic. It was the yellow sleeve of the jacket in the snow that caught my attention when I discovered the body earlier."

As she was talking, Ellie had gotten up from the table and crossed the room to the coat closet off the foyer, followed closely by Cord and the deputy. She opened the closet door, lifted the yellow jacket off the hook on the back of the door and held it out as if it had some kind of contagious disease.

63

Cord didn't wait for the deputy. He took the jacket from Ellie and looked it over. This changed everything.

"Miss Nelson, you stay put. Don't go out anywhere. I still need to talk with you; I'll be back."

Ellie was surprised by the harshness of his tone, but before she could respond, he quickly turned, opened the door, and walked out of the house.

The deputy seemed unsure as to whether he needed to follow Cord or finish taking Ellie's statement. Apparently following Cord won out. He muttered a quick apology to Ellie and said he'd have to finish her statement later. Then, he, too, walked out the door and broke into a sprint toward Cord's SUV.

Ellie stepped out on the front porch. She could see that the deputy was not going to catch up with Cord. Cord was already in his SUV and backing out the driveway. The deputy was waving his arms and shouting at Cord to stop. As the black SUV continued backing out of the driveway, the deputy began talking into his radio.

CHAPTER 6

Cord saw the deputy waving at him as he began backing out the driveway, but he ignored him. He backed onto the county road and then drove in the direction where he had last seen the Sheriff. The deputy had obviously radioed ahead because the Sheriff stepped to the center of the road and held out his hand as Cord's SUV approached the crest of the hill.

Cord stopped, and the Sheriff came around to his window. Cord pushed the button and the black-tinted window slid down to reveal an obviously annoyed Sheriff.

"Now, what do you think you're doing? My deputy tells me you interrupted his interview and got all excited about a jacket of Miss Nelson's. You want to tell me what's going on?"

Cord had no intention of letting the Sheriff in on what he was really investigating. But he wanted to get a look at the dead man and he knew that meant he was going to have to have the Sheriff's cooperation.

"Just another coincidence, I'm sure. But the bureau likes to have all the i's dotted and the t's crossed. Miss Nelson says her jacket is just like the one your dead guy was wearing. On the chance that Miss Nelson is somehow connected to this incident, I'd like to see the dead guy's personal effects."

The Sheriff's eyes bored into Cord. "Any reason, Special Agent Sinclair, you think there would be a connection with Miss Nelson?"

"None that I can think of," said Cord. "Like I told you earlier, this is just a routine interview with Miss Nelson. But my report is going to have to include the murder and Miss Nelson's knowledge of the victim. Since Miss Nelson mentioned the similarities in their jogging apparel, I'll have to follow up in order for my report to be complete. As I said, all the i's dotted and the t's crossed."

"Well, that's some mighty fancy dancing there, Special Agent Sinclair, and I don't think you're even close to telling me what you're doing here. But, let me tell you something.

"That jacket," he said, pointing to the rumpled yellow jacket that Cord had tossed into the passenger seat, "is one of a thousand just like it. My wife has one and she bought one for me. They offered them at the Adidas Outlet store for $5 apiece. They went like hotcakes. Every other person down here probably has one. I don't like coincidences any better than you, but unless you know something I don't, my investigation is going to focus on Doug Withers. And I can't see any connection to Miss Nelson at the moment other than the fact that she found the body."

The Sheriff took out a pad of paper and pen and began writing. "Here's where the Doc is. I'll call him and let him know you're coming by. I also wrote down my office and home numbers. Call me, Special Agent Sinclair, when you are done with the Doc." With that he tore the sheet of paper from the pad, handed it to Cord and motioned him to drive on.

Cord gave the Sheriff a brief nod. He pushed the button to close the window and reached over and turned the knob for the heater fan to full power. The open window had allowed the cold winter air into the car and Cord was cold. He had left the Nelson home in a hurry and his overcoat was still draped over the back of one of the dining room chairs. He didn't want to take the time to go back for it now. It'd just have to wait until he was finished with the medical examiner.

Cord plugged the address the Sheriff had given him into the SUV's GPS system and began to go over the morning's events in his head. What should have been a fairly routine interview had turned into something else entirely. And Cord had a bad feeling about this new information. He needed to see the dead guy's jacket and check out the man's physical characteristics. He hadn't gotten a close enough look as the E.M.T.s were removing the body.

He hadn't been too far off the truth with what he had told the Sheriff. He definitely was going to have to put this in his report. He really hoped he was wrong. He really hoped that the dead guy was a big muscular guy, about six feet and 200 pounds. According to her file, Ellie Nelson was five foot five and 130 pounds. A clear picture of Ellie formed in Cord's mind and he let out an involuntary sigh. Yep,

5' 5" was just about right, he could picture pulling her close and almost feel her head laying against his chest snuggled just below his chin.

"Whoa," Cord said to himself. "You have no business going there. Focus, Sinclair."

He was saved from any other thoughts along those lines when his GPS announced, "You have reached your destination."

Cord looked around hastily and pulled into the next driveway on the right. The driveway led into a parking lot that sat in front of what was obviously the area's hospital. Once again Cord was sorry he had left his overcoat at the Nelson house. There were no parking spaces open near the building entrance. Cord wound through the lot and finally found a space about six rows back.

Cord steeled himself for the cold that hit him as soon as he opened the SUV's door. The cold bit hard into his face and his blazer did nothing to block out the stiff breeze that was whipping across the parking lot.

Sprinting as best he could, Cord weaved through the parked cars while trying to keep his footing in the snow. The lot had obviously been too full for any snowplow to make much headway in clearing away the foot of snow. He reached the front entrance to the hospital and pulled open the doors. He was grateful to reach the warmth of the hospital lobby and headed straight for the reception desk in the center of the room.

He waited impatiently in front of the receptionist who was on the phone. She glanced up at Cord and raised her index finger, indicating she would be with him in a minute. Cord waited while the receptionist gave directions to reach the hospital. The caller obviously had no familiarity with the area as the woman had to repeat everything three times and had to spell out the names of the streets.

Cord had just about decided to try to find the doctor on his own when the receptionist hung up the phone and looked up at Cord with a tired but pleasant smile.

"I'm sorry to have kept you waiting. How can I help you?

"I'm here to consult with Doctor Wheeler. He's expecting me. Can you direct me to the morgue?"

"Take the elevators right down the hall there and push B2. Exit to your left and then follow the hallway clear to the steel door at the end. There's an intercom there. Press the green button and repeat there what you told me. Someone will buzz you through and escort you back to the morgue."

Cord followed the instructions the receptionist had given him and was buzzed into another hallway where he was met by a young orderly.

"Follow me, please. Doctor Wheeler is just finishing up with Mr. Withers."

They walked down a short hallway to another steel door where the orderly keyed in a sequence of numbers on a keypad beside the door. The door slid open with a slight whooshing sound and the orderly motioned him through the doorway.

Cord stopped once inside and took a quick look around. The room was typical of most hospital morgues, although smaller than some Cord had seen. Unfortunately, he had seen too many. But that was unavoidable in his line of work. There were about a dozen steel vaults along one wall, with various cabinets, computers, and other medical equipment lining the others. In the middle of the room were three steel tables. Doctor Wheeler, his back to Cord, was standing by the center table which contained the body of Doug Withers.

The orderly said something to Doctor Wheeler that Cord couldn't hear. The doctor pulled off a set of clear rubber gloves, dropped them in a hazardous waste bin near the table, and then walked toward Cord.

"I'm just finishing up here. The Sheriff said you wanted to take a look at Withers personal effects?'

"That's right. But I also have a couple of questions about Withers."

"What kind of questions. I've completed my preliminary investigation and I'm sure you know I can't share any results with you. You'll have to go through the Sheriff for that. The M.E. probably won't do the full autopsy until Monday or Tuesday."

As the two were talking, Cord had been casually easing his way toward the steel table where he could get a little closer look at Withers. Just as Cord had feared, Withers was on the short side. He also had a slight build. Not that the guy was skinny. Lean would be the way to describe him.

"Can you tell me how tall Withers is?"

"Sure," said Doc Wheeler, "I can tell you that much. He's just a bit under five feet six inches. Look, I need to finish up here. Go on over to Jenkins there and he'll let you look at Withers things. They're already bagged and tagged so that'll have to do."

Cord went over to the orderly who was waiting by a counter top where several plastic bags were lying. Cord pointed to the bag containing the yellow jacket and Jenkins picked it up and handed it to him. It was definitely a match with the one that Ellie Nelson had. He had seen enough; he didn't like what he was seeing.

He called a thanks to Doctor Wheeler and told the orderly he could find his own way out. He was feeling a bit of urgency about getting back to talk with Ellie Nelson. She and Doug Withers were about the same height and build. Withers had been wearing a yellow jacket just like one that Ellie had worn the two previous days. The hood on the jacket had been pulled up and tied tightly, exposing only Wither's face. From a distance, someone who had seen Ellie jogging in the yellow jacket might have mistaken Withers for her.

If Ellie Nelson was the target, it was entirely possible that she would be in danger when information about the shooting became public and the shooter learned about the mistake. Hit men tended to want to complete their contracts, either to maintain a certain reputation or to prevent any backlash from the person who hired them.

Cord's first instinct was to get back to Ellie Nelson. He had an overwhelming sense that she was in danger and that he needed to protect her, wanted to protect her. He realized that his reaction was a bit over the top considering he had just met the woman and she was a person of interest in a public corruption case being investigated by the F.B.I. It was also irrational to think that she couldn't possibly be part of the corruption. He hadn't even gotten into questioning her about her knowledge of Jack Manetti. Cord had good instincts and could usually read people well. Maybe he was only seeing what he wanted to see. But the fact was, Cord liked Ellie Nelson, liked her a lot. Truth be told, he liked her more than he should. His gut was telling him there was no way she could be mixed up with the likes of Jack Manetti.

Although he wanted to get back to Ellie Nelson as soon as he could, he also knew that he had a little more time before the death of Doug Withers began to hit the media. The fact it was a Sunday helped. It would probably be sometime Monday before this local shooting hit the airwaves in either Kansas City or St. Louis.

It was time to call his boss in the Kansas City field office and let him know the situation with Ellie Nelson had changed. As he was driving, Cord had been keeping an eye out for a Starbuck's he had passed earlier on his way to the hospital morgue.

A few minutes later, the Starbuck's appeared on the left side of the road. Cord pulled into the drive-thru and ordered a tall Café Mocha. He'd gotten hooked on the drink about a year earlier during a visit to his parents. It was his mother's favorite and she had a habit of just ordering everyone the same drink as hers, because she didn't want to have to remember all the different variations that were possible when ordering at a Starbucks.

Cord picked up his drink at the drive-thru window, paid the barista and left a dollar tip in the jar sitting on the window ledge. He pulled around the Starbucks building and parked in the adjacent lot. He took a sip of the coffee. The hot, chocolaty coffee helped to take the last of the chill off. Cord had had the SUVs heater going full blast since leaving the hospital. The wind had kicked up as Cord had worked his way from the hospital entrance back to the SUV and he might as well have been bare-chested for all the good his blazer had been in keeping the cold out.

He took another sip of the coffee and then pulled out his cell phone. He paged down through his contact list until he found his boss's cell number. Cord had been working with Walter Dunlap for three years. The Kansas City Special Agent in Charge, or S.A.C. for short, was a no-nonsense kind of guy that expected results from his agents. He also expected the agents to work on their own initiative and didn't try to micro-manage.

Cord had quickly earned Dunlap's trust and respect and it was mutual. He knew the S.A.C. wouldn't like being interrupted on a Sunday, but he also knew that he'd want to be made aware of what was happening at The Lake. Besides, Cord was going to need the S.A.C. to approve some additional resources for the task force. If he was right, then this murder added a new level to their investigation into the Manetti operations. He wanted to get the team looking through surveillance tapes to see if they could pick up anything about a possible contract being put out in the area.

When the S.A.C. answered his cell, Cord quickly filled him in on what had happened at the Nelson house and that he believed Ellie Nelson had been the intended target. After listening to everything Cord had to say, Walter Dunlap gave Cord the authorization he needed to try to get the information to confirm his suspicions. Dunlap told Cord that he would coordinate with the Denver office, but until advised otherwise, Cord was to go back to the Nelson house and complete the original assignment to interview Ellie Nelson. If Dunlap hadn't gotten back to him by the time he was finished with the interview, he was to get a room at a local hotel and await further instructions. Dunlap also agreed that they weren't going to bring the local Sheriff into the loop until they were able to confirm that Ellie Nelson had been the target rather than Doug Withers.

CHAPTER 7

Ellie looked out the dining room window and let out a sigh of relief. The morning's events were finally winding down. The Sheriff's deputy had just left after having come back to finish up Ellie's statement. She'd had to repeat everything she had said before and then agreed to stop by the Sheriff's office the next day to sign the statement after it had been prepared from the deputy's notes.

Ellie heard an audible grumble and realized it was her stomach growling. It was no wonder. She hadn't eaten any breakfast and it was now one o'clock. All the coffee she had had was starting to burn a hole in her stomach. It might be afternoon, but breakfast was what sounded good to Ellie. She knew she had all the makings for a veggie omelet and her mouth started to water. She was just about to head into the kitchen, when she saw an unfamiliar car pulling into the driveway. The car might have been unfamiliar, but the occupants weren't.

Ellie sighed again, walked into the great room and started toward the far end of the house. She had only gotten a few steps when the door from the garage flew open.

"Eleanor!"

"Mother," Ellie said, closing the distance rapidly and giving her mother a hug and a kiss on the cheek, "What are you doing here?"

Evelyn Nelson had taken a step back but was still holding Ellie's shoulders. She gave Ellie a hard once over and seemed to come to a conclusion. She looked briefly back over her shoulder as Ellie's father came through the garage door.

"She's okay, Howard."

Howard Nelson stepped up to Ellie and hugged her gently. The morning seemed to catch up with Ellie a bit and for a moment she was a little girl, sagging into her dad's arms, ready for him to make everything all better. Ellie's dad continued to hold

By P. L. Gertner

her for a moment more and then gave her a reassuring pat on the back as he released her.

"Of course, she's okay, Evelyn. Aren't you, Princess?"

Ellie smiled at her dad's use of his pet name for her. It had been awhile since she had heard him call her that. It made Ellie feel good and bad at the same time. Good because it brought back really fond memories, but bad because Ellie realized she didn't see her folks often enough and here they both were, obviously very worried about her.

"I'm okay, really. I'm sorry if I worried you. It's just that I've been trying to sort things out."

"It's time you told us what's going on, Ellie, starting with why there is crime scene tape strung up beside our driveway."

"I will, Mother, just as soon as I eat something. I haven't had anything all morning and I was just about to make myself an omelet. Can I make one for both of you, also?"

"Actually, an omelet sounds good. We didn't want to stop on the way, even though we were making very good time. But why don't you just sit down and let me make the omelets. Your father can tell you about his new toy. Then, after we eat, no more

80

excuses; I want to know everything that's happened and why you are here in the first place."

Ellie stood looking dumbfounded at her mother. While she had been talking, Ellie's father had helped her mother off with her coat and was walking toward the closet in the foyer. Ellie noticed that even he stopped dead in his tracks and looked back at his wife.

They were both used to Evelyn taking charge. What they weren't used to is Evelyn saying she was going to cook. There was a standing joke in the family that Evelyn didn't know there was a room called a kitchen. She and Ellie's father mostly ate out, or sometimes her father cooked. Ellie could not recall seeing her mother in the kitchen anytime in recent memory.

"Oh, stop, both of you. Just because I don't cook doesn't mean I can't. I happen to make a superb omelet. Sit, both of you, this won't take long."

That was the end of that discussion. There was no arguing with Evelyn once she had taken charge and Ellie was secretly pleased. Although she would never admit it, this was as close as it came to being babied and it wasn't all bad under the circumstances. In fact, Ellie kind of liked it. She had been on her own for a long time and was used to doing things herself, but it was kind of comforting to have her mom and dad here. Maybe that's what she had needed all along. Ellie made the decision she was going to tell her folks everything. Maybe they'd even have some ideas about what she should do.

But that could wait just a bit. Right now, Ellie was fully enjoying watching her mother move about in the kitchen preparing the omelets. As her dad came to the table and sat down, Ellie turned to him with a big smile.

"So, tell me about your new toy, Dad. You must have been flying. Were the roads clear? You must have made it here in under three hours."

"Porsche Cayenne Turbo S," Howard Nelson said, grinning like a kid. "Big V8 engine that'll go 0 to 60 almost as fast as the 911."

"Did you trade in the 911?"

"Oh no, that's still my favorite. But your mother talked me into getting an SUV. She said it'd be better for weather just like this. I don't think the Cayenne was exactly what she had in mind, but she can't deny it's got all the safety features she wanted. Can I help it that it's also a screamer? This was the first time I'd had it out on the highway for any length of time.

What a blast. The roads were mostly dry until we hit Jefferson City and I had to make myself keep it under 90."

Evelyn was in the kitchen pretending to ignore the conversation. But Ellie thought she could see a hint of a smile. Her mother was just plating the omelets and Ellie jumped up to lend a hand.

Ellie pulled out one of the drawers and grabbed a set of silverware for each of them. Opening another drawer, Ellie took out three cloth napkins and carried them to the table. Ellie usually just grabbed a paper towel off the roll on the counter, but she knew her mother always preferred using the cloth napkins. Evelyn didn't believe in "making do." She always said it only took a few extra seconds to do something the right way. So, there was simply no reason not to do so.

"I've got some orange juice in the refrigerator," Ellie said. "I know it's not fresh squeezed, Mom, but I think it'll go well with the omelets."

"That'll be fine, Ellie. Then please sit and enjoy your omelet before it gets cold."

Ellie filled three glasses with the orange juice, brought them to the table and then sat down and took her first bite of the omelet her mother had made.

"Wow, Mom, this is terrific."

And it was. For several minutes no one said a word. The three of them were content to simply sit and enjoy the wonderful omelet. The eggs were light and fluffy and were folded expertly over a mixture of tomatoes, mushrooms and onions. The eggs were then topped with a layer of melted sharp white cheddar cheese. It was all seasoned perfectly and would not have seemed out of place if it were being served in a five-star restaurant instead of the Nelson Lake House.

They all seemed to finish at the same time and Ellie's father stood.

"Okay, your mother cooked, I'll do the cleanup."

Ellie started to argue, but her father held up a hand.

"It'll just take a minute. I'm just going to rinse things off and put them in the dishwasher. Why don't you two go on into the great room? Don't start your story until I get in there though."

Ellie and her mother stood up from the table and it was then her mother noticed the overcoat draped over the chair.

"Howard," she called over her shoulder into the kitchen, "didn't I see you take your coat to the closet?"

"Yes, it's not mine."

"Ellie?"

"Oh, that belongs to the F.B.I. agent that was here. He rushed out of the house earlier with my yellow jacket. He said he'd be coming back."

"What yellow jacket? And why would he be wearing your yellow jacket instead of this lovely overcoat? It's an Armani. An F.B.I. agent who wears Armani? Cashmere. 38 Long. Any jacket of yours couldn't possibly have fit."

"I didn't say he was wearing my jacket, Mother. He was carrying it. He seemed to think it was important that the dead guy had a jacket like mine and he just grabbed it and ran out the door."

"Dead guy? What dead guy?"

"Howard, leave those things. We'll clean up later. I want to know what's been going on and I want to know now."

CHAPTER 8

E velyn moved into the great room, expecting Ellie and her father to follow. And follow they did. Evelyn seated herself on one end of the contemporary sectional that dominated the room. Howard sat down next to her and Ellie was just getting ready to sit in the arm chair facing them, when the doorbell rang.

Since Ellie was still standing, she said she would get it. She walked into the foyer and gave a peak out the window that ran alongside the door. Her heart did that little skip a beat thing again as she saw Cord Sinclair standing on the porch on the other side of the door. She opened the door and, before she couldn't even say hello, Cord stepped inside and said, "We have to talk."

"Uh, sure, but..."

"I mean it. No stalling this time."

Before Ellie could say anything more, Ellie's parents walked into the foyer.

"Eleanor, is there a problem?"

"No, Mother, no problem. Mother, Father, this is Special Agent Cordell Sinclair, with the F.B.I. Special Agent Sinclair, these are my parents, Howard and Evelyn Nelson."

Cord was surprised to see Ellie's parents. He had been so focused on Ellie that he hadn't noticed the people sitting in the great room beyond the foyer. But he was even more surprised with what happened next.

At the mention of the F.B.I. agent's name, Ellie's parents had exchanged a funny look. Ellie's father extended his hand and as he and Cord shook hands, Ellie's father said, "Would that be Cordell Weston Sinclair, uh, the fourth, I believe?"

Cord stood wordless and simply nodded. It usually took a lot to surprise him, but he was literally dumbfounded. It got worse.

Howard and Evelyn Nelson exchanged another look and then they both cried out in delight.

"Cubby!"

Ellie had been watching all this in amazement, looking first at Cord, then to her parents, then back to Cord. When her parents had shouted out "Cubby," Cord had visibly winced.

Ellie's mother then grabbed Cord by the hand and led him into the great room.

"How is your mother? I haven't seen Catherine in years. I'm so sorry to say we've lost touch. We used to have a marvelous time together didn't we, Howard?"

"Evelyn, let go of the boy. I believe you're embarrassing him and he obviously has no idea what you're talking about. And there's no reason he should. What, he must have been about five when we saw him last. I'll hazard a guess no one calls him Cubby any more. Have a seat, Son."

Cord sat down, still looking a bit dazed and looking at Ellie like she should jump in and rescue him. But Ellie was as clueless as he was about how his folks knew him. Ellie's father went on to explain that he had worked with Cord's father early on in his career and the two families had socialized on many occasions. When Howard had left Boston to take a position in Kansas City, they had stayed in touch via phone calls, cards and the like. But as these things go, the communications became further and further apart until now only Christmas cards were exchanged, with Evelyn and Catherine adding brief family updates along with holiday wishes.

"Let's see, your mother didn't mention anything in last year's Christmas card. So, I'm assuming you're still single, Cub...er, Cord. You know, Ellie's never been married. She's always working..."

Ellie had sort of been enjoying Cord's obvious discomfort. But she didn't like where her mother was going with the conversation now. She quickly interrupted, and Cord shot her a look of gratitude.

"Mother, I don't believe Special Agent Sinclair is here to renew old acquaintances."

"Mr. and Mrs. Nelson, your daughter is right. I'm here officially. In fact, although the family connection you've mentioned might pose some complications, I don't believe there is a conflict of interest. I need to interview your daughter with regard to an investigation into organized crime being worked jointly between the Denver and Kansas City field offices."

"Does my daughter need legal counsel present?"

"That is certainly her right, Ma'am, as I'm sure she knows. But she isn't under arrest and she hasn't been read her rights. At this time, we are just trying to determine to what extent your daughter is involved in an ongoing investigation. After this morning's events, I believe it's absolutely urgent that we learn what your daughter knows."

With that all eyes turned to where Ellie sat. She had already decided to tell her parents everything and she realized that as Cord had been speaking, she had made another decision as well. She looked at her parents and then at Cord.

"I'm not sure why you think this morning's events have anything to do with it, but I was just going to fill my parents in. You might as well get out your tape recorder. I don't want to have to tell it twice."

Both Ellie's mother and Cord seemed about to say something, but Ellie cut them short.

"Just hold any questions or comments until I'm through."

With that Ellie went into her Deputy District Attorney mode. This was the side of Ellie that her co-workers saw. This was a tough, no-nonsense, capable woman that knew exactly what needed to be done and what needed to be said.

Ellie's parents noticed the change in her demeanor and they actually relaxed. This was what they had wanted to see. When they had first entered the house, Ellie had seemed vulnerable and confused. It had been disconcerting. Ellie had always been confident and self-assured, and they didn't like it that something had shaken that confidence. But she seemed to have snapped back.

Ellie gave a curt nod to Cord now who pushed the button on his recorder and placed it on the coffee table in front of Ellie.

"Special Agent Cordell W. Sinclair interview with Eleanor J. Nelson. Also present are Howard and Evelyn Nelson, parents of Eleanor Nelson. Miss Nelson has indicated she would like to make an initial statement. Go ahead, Miss Nelson."

"It all started about two weeks ago, with what was originally thought to be a suicide."

Ellie went on to explain how Stephen Lindsey, a prominent Denver attorney, had been found dead on the sidewalk on Seventeenth Street in downtown Denver. A witness on the street said it had looked like the man had jumped from the top floor of a six-story parking garage. The idea that the attorney had committed suicide was quickly refuted after detectives found evidence of a struggle on the roof and indications that the attorney's car had been searched. When they tried to do a follow up the next day with the witness, they found the contact information for the witness was false.

The Denver Police began to recanvas the surrounding businesses and street vendors and got lucky. One of the hot dog vendors remembered seeing a guy come out of the parking garage shortly after Lindsey had fallen from the roof. He said he didn't think of it before because the guy was always walking around the downtown area. The vendor said the guy was usually strung out but would occasionally buy a hot dog from him. He said people in the area called him Harpo because he had curly blonde hair like that old Marx brother.

With that kind of description, it wasn't tough for the detectives to locate Harpo and take him in for questioning. They didn't even get through reading the Miranda rights when Harpo confessed he'd done it. He said he'd broken into Lindsey's BMW, but that Lindsey had caught him in the act. Lindsey had jumped out at him and they had started to fight. He said he had given Lindsey a push and hadn't realized that they were so close to the railing. Harpo said Lindsey went over the rail before he could grab him. He said it was an accident and he panicked and just got out of there as quick as he could.

The case had been given to Ellie to prosecute. They were charging Harpo, one Randolph Ross, with murder in the second degree, while in the commission of a crime. But while Ellie was putting together the case to present for sentencing, she began to notice some inconsistencies. Things just weren't adding up.

From an interview with the receptionist at the victim's law firm, detectives learned that Lindsey always carried a briefcase with him. The briefcase was not found near the victim, in his car, or at his home. Harpo never mentioned anything about a briefcase.

During one description of his fight with Lindsey, Harpo stated that he had pulled a knife on Lindsey. Later, when the detectives were recording the official statement, Harpo said he had pulled a gun. Neither statement matched the original one where Harpo only mentioned pushing Lindsey. A search of Harpo's apartment turned up no weapon of any kind.

Disturbed with the inconsistencies in Harpo's statement, Ellie had taken another look at the case file. It was then she had noticed that a bullet key chain had been entered into evidence. She had a hunch that the key chain might be a key piece of evidence. Ellie explained how although she hadn't given Hanover any details, she had told him she had potentially found something that might mean they would need to reopen the case. It was then that Hanover had told her in no uncertain terms that case was closed and she was to drop it.

It just wasn't in Ellie's nature to leave any avenue open. So, she had ignored Hanover's order and contacted the lead detective to determine if the key chain was still in the evidence locker. Since Harpo had confessed, the case was also closed as far as the D.P.D. detective was concerned. Like Ellie, he thought there was something off about the case, but there wasn't anything he could do about it. The procedure was for the D.A.s Victim's Advocate to return personal items to remaining family members. So, the detective had no problem with giving the key chain to Ellie who said she would see that it got to the Victim's Advocate.

Someone had told Hanover that she had gone ahead with her investigation and he had fired her the next day, confiscating both the key chain and her laptop.

"You were fired?" Ellie's mom blurted out.

Ellie had been talking non-stop for a half hour and her mother's interruption had come out at a good time. There was actually more to tell but Ellie wasn't quite ready to tell everything she knew at the moment. She was still working a few things out in her own head.

"Can we take a break, Special Agent Sinclair?" Ellie asked.

Cord hesitated for a moment but then hit the button to turn the recorder off.

"We can take a break, yes. But I would actually like to get the answer to your mother's question and I'd like to ask you not to discuss that until we go back on the record."

At that, Evelyn stood up and glared at Cord. "You can ask all you want. But, there's nothing to prevent Eleanor from talking about anything she wants. She is not under arrest. In fact, you have given us nothing in the way of an explanation as to why you are here in the first place, other than a vague reference to an organized crime task force. Eleanor's statement was voluntary. We can change that in a heartbeat if you want to start playing hardball, Special Agent Sinclair."

Ellie gave a brief smile and a slight nod to her mother. She was right of course. There was no reason for Ellie to give a statement. She hadn't even asked Cord in what context he was there to see her. She had agreed to an interview and had given a statement as much to hear the story out loud as to gauge how much of what she said was already known to the F.B.I.

Ellie was not a stranger to the F.B.I. Because she had prosecuted Jack Manetti on two occasions, she had become very familiar with a couple of the agents in the Denver office, and had been to various business and charitable functions where the Denver Special Agent in Charge was also in attendance. Organized crime cases were of special interest to the F.B.I. because of the Racketeer Influenced and Corrupt Organizations Act, better known as the R.I.C.O. Act. They hadn't been too pleased when her Manetti cases had disintegrated. But the fallout from those had died down and she would have wondered why they were showing up now if it hadn't been for what she had glimpsed in Lindsey's files. She really only had two questions about the F.B.I. involvement. One, why hadn't a Denver agent shown up at the door, instead of one out of the Kansas City office? And, two, why hadn't it happened sooner?

Hanover had the Lindsey files and there hadn't been a peep out of Denver about anyone reopening the Lindsey case. And she would have known. She and her friend Lisa had been talking on the phone and exchanging emails. Lisa had said Hanover had been on the warpath ever since Ellie had left. Lots of urgent phone calls, slammed doors and a very short fuse had everyone just trying to keep out of his line of fire. But Lisa hadn't mentioned the F.B.I. showing up either. So, obviously Hanover had not shared the Lindsey files with them. If that was the case, Ellie took back her two questions. If the F.B.I. didn't know about Lindsey's tie to Manetti, she only had one question. Why were they here at all?

Ellie broke the silence that had descended on the room after her mother had thrown down her gauntlet, so to speak.

"Mother is right, Special Agent Sinclair. To a large extent everything I've said so far was as much to bring my parents up to date as to why I'm here as it was to provide information to you. To my knowledge, nothing I've said here today warrants a visit to me by the F.B.I. Perhaps you'd like to make a statement of your own?"

With that all eyes were on Cord. He paused for a moment just to give himself some time to process the information Ellie had just given them. Unfortunately, it only added to the theory he was developing. And not in a good way.

He knew Ellie hadn't told him everything and he wasn't quite sure if her mother really didn't know Ellie had been fired or whether it was just a ploy to help Ellie cut off her statement. This family was something else. Intelligent and fiercely loyal. He had the feeling if Mr. Nelson thought Cord was endangering his family, the man might just take him on...and give him a run for his money from the looks of him. He wasn't sure he really wanted to go there, and he was certain he was going to make a call to his own mother in the near future for a little background.

After a couple more minutes when no one spoke, Cord made his decision. He wasn't sure his boss would agree. But he just decided to lay it all out for the Nelsons. After all, they were practically family, according to Evelyn Nelson. Maybe a little give and take was in order.

"Okay. Here's the deal. I'm going to go outside of policy and I'm going to tell you about the case I'm working. When I'm through, Ellie is going to tell us whatever it was that she was holding back."

Cord held up a hand as Ellie and her mother both started to object.

"Let me finish. Let's drop the Special Agent Sinclair when the recorder isn't on. Please call me, Cord. And no one, I repeat, no one, will ever mention the name Cubby again! Deal?"

Cord's last requirement was presented with a bit of desperation, his voice rising to a plea-filled crescendo at the end. For just a beat, no one said anything. But the tension that had been in the room previously was suddenly gone. Then they all broke out at once, laughing.

As the laughter died down, Cord looked first at Mr. Nelson.

"Deal," Howard said as he nodded.

"Deal," Evelyn said as Cord turned to look at her.

Ellie hesitated for just a moment. But, she, too, had made her decision. Truth be known, she had probably made it as soon as she had first seen him on her doorstep. She didn't want to hide anything from this man.

"Deal," Ellie said, still smiling.

CHAPTER 9

E veryone seemed to relax and settled back in their chairs as Cord began talking.

"As I said earlier, the F.B.I. has an investigation in work that deals with organized crime activities in Denver and Kansas City. The old mob leader in Kansas City, Gino Russo, passed away a few months ago and his second in command has taken over the business. The new boss's last name will no doubt be familiar to you, Ellie. It's Manetti. Tommy Manetti. His brother is Jack Manetti, who just so happened to be the head of the crime family in Denver."

"I'm well acquainted with Jack Manetti," Ellie interrupted. "He has figured prominently in several cases we've had in Denver. But he's never been convicted."

Cord nodded. "We have the same problem in Kansas City when it comes to Tommy Manetti. Evidence and witnesses have a tendency to disappear if we get close. Right around the same time that Tommy Manetti took over the crime family in Kansas City, a prominent lawyer died."

"Rob Carter," said Evelyn, "I remember when that happened. It was ruled a suicide. He jumped from a downtown parking garage."

Cord saw Ellie's eyes go wide.

"Yes, it was ruled a suicide. But we didn't like the coincidence. Rob Carter was Gino Russo's lawyer. We'd had a tip from one of our informants that there was a hit going down right around that time. The informant didn't know who the target was, but he knew the order for the hit had come out of Denver rather than from Kansas City. We began coordinating with the Denver field office to see if our suicide might have been a murder. We've been monitoring the activities of both Manetti brothers. One of the Bureau's prime directives is to combat organized crime and the consolidation of control for two major cities under one family is not something we like to see."

While listening to Cord, part of Ellie's mind began spinning. Some of the pieces were finally clicking into place. She hadn't known about the suicide in Kansas City. She wasn't sure what the connection was between her dead lawyer in Denver and the dead lawyer in Kansas City. But she knew there was one. That connection would explain why the flash drive that had been in Lindsey's possession contained what appeared to be a rundown of illegal activities not only in Denver but in Kansas City as well. At least that was the way Ellie had interpreted the cryptic notes in the files.

Ellie had only skimmed the files on the flash drive before Hanover had taken both it and her laptop. But from what little she did see and, if she had interpreted the information in the files correctly, she could understand why someone might have killed Lindsey to get it. The problem, of course, was that although they had killed Lindsey, they had not recognized the key chain fob for what it was and missed getting the information they had been looking for. And that information was now in the hands of the Denver District Attorney. What she couldn't figure out was how or why Lindsey had the files in the first place. Ellie had been involved in several of the cases that had been started and then aborted against Jack Manetti. And she had never come across any mention of Lindsey in connection with Manetti. But, the similarities between the deaths of the two lawyers were just too much of a coincidence.

There had to be something that tied Lindsey to the Manetti's, possibly that tie was Rob Carter. That hadn't been the only thing that had been troubling Ellie. The other was that she knew that the Denver District Attorney had had possession of the flash drive for over a week, yet nothing had come of it. And Ellie would have known if anything was in the works. Her friend Lisa would have been on the phone in a heartbeat. There should have been lots of effort going on to analyze the shorthand that had been used throughout most of the files, followed by detailed investigations to confirm the information. There were only two possible reasons that Ellie could think of to explain why there was no apparent activity from the D.A.'s office as a result of Lindsey's flash drive.

Some of the shorthand in the files seemed to point to someone in the D.A.'s office passing information to Manetti. So, either Hanover was handling the investigation himself to discover who that person was. Or, the person providing information to Manetti was Hanover. Ellie hadn't wanted to think that the latter was true. But it was the only thing that fit. The only thing that made sense for firing her for pursuing the Lindsey investigation. It only made sense if Lindsey was connected to Manetti and Hanover was a part of seeing that connection was never made. She had been hoping that she was wrong and that any day she would hear that Hanover was bringing charges against Jack Manetti. But it had been over a week now and nothing had happened. Maybe the answer for what to do was sitting right in front of her. Maybe it was time to tell Cord what she suspected and let the F.B.I. handle it from there.

As Ellie's full attention came back to Cord, she realized that he had stopped talking and that he, along with her mother and father were all looking at her. It registered somewhere in her brain that Cord had just asked her a question. Something about the Manetti cases she had handled. She snapped back to the conversation.

"Wait just a minute, Cord. Or is it Special Agent Sinclair asking that question?"

Cord took a moment to answer. He was about to do something that was totally against the rules. Even he was amazed at what he was going to do. If his instincts were wrong, he was potentially risking his career. But Cord had never been so certain of anything as he was that Ellie Nelson had no involvement with the Manetti family. He had only known her for a few hours, but he couldn't deny the effect she had had on him. It was uncanny really how clearly he could read her in such a short time.

He hadn't missed the fact that Ellie hadn't been totally focused on the background he had been giving. But he also knew that her brain wasn't spinning to come up with a story or a way to spin the facts to cover herself. He could almost see a light bulb going off and could feel her working through a problem and a solution. He'd also noticed that she had visibly stiffened when he had asked her to tell him why she thought Jack Manetti had never been convicted for any crime in Denver. He didn't have a choice really. He had to pursue the question and he had to get the answer on the record. But he had made his decision on just how he was going to go about it.

"Okay, calm down a minute, Ellie. I'm going to go way out of bounds here and give you the whole picture. Then I'm going to turn on the recorder and ask you the question again. I need some answers and I think you just decided a minute ago to give them to me."

Ellie studied Cord intently. She had to admit she was more offended that it was Cord asking her the question, rather than about the question itself. There was no denying the implication in the question. The implication was that Ellie had somehow botched the Manetti cases she had handled. Here she was about to trust the man with what she knew, and he was sitting there practically accusing her of being on Manetti's payroll.

But, looking at Cord now, Ellie knew the stress of recent events had made her overreact. She did trust Cord. She knew in her very core that he would do anything in his power to protect her. Ellie had learned to take care of herself and was proud of it. However, she couldn't deny the unsettling feeling that had been growing for over a week now. And she was beginning to look at the morning's event in a different light. Ellie was almost certain that she needed protection.

Ellie let out an audible sigh and relaxed a bit in her chair.

"I'm sorry, Cord. It's been a long day—a long few weeks, actually. You're right. I do have some information for you. And I think I may need your help. I can probably guess at a lot of what you were about to say, and I don't want you to risk anything because of me. You can ask me the question again. Now. On the record."

Evelyn and Howard Nelson had been watching the exchange between Ellie and Cord with considerable interest. They, too, had been concerned when Cord had stopped providing background and had instead asked a question that had obviously upset their daughter. A question that had Evelyn ready to jump back into lawyer mode. But it wasn't lost on either of them that there was something going on, on a whole different level, between Ellie and Cord. More out of routine than actual concern, Evelyn spoke up.

"Are you sure that's a good idea, Ellie? Maybe you should let Cord give you a few more details."

"It's okay, Mother. I know what I'm doing. Turn on the recorder, Cord. Let's get started."

Cord once again pressed the button on his recorder and placed it in the center of the table.

"Miss Nelson, during the last three years you were the lead prosecutor for two separate cases brought against John, aka Jack, Manetti. Neither of those cases made it to the courtroom even though local law enforcement felt the evidence was strong enough for a conviction. Can you tell me why those cases never went to trial?"

"First, let me say that, while local law enforcement always feels they have strong enough evidence for a conviction, that is simply not always the case. Having said that, however, I have to agree with them in these instances. I was confident with both cases that I would get a conviction. "

"So, what happened, Miss Nelson?"

"The first case was against Jack Manetti for first degree murder. We had a witness, a janitor actually, who was in the wrong place at the right time. He overheard Jack Manetti giving an order to kill a local businessman. I use the term businessman loosely. The man's business was drugs and by all indications he had begun cutting into what Manetti felt was his territory. Two days before the trial, the witness disappeared. Without his testimony, we had no case, and we were forced to drop it."

"The second case was not actually against Jack Manetti, personally. It was against Zach Lando, who had been rising fast in the Manetti organization. His rise was due in great part to the fact that he was married to Manetti's baby sister, Maria. He wasn't known for any great intelligence, but he apparently was good to Maria and Manetti took care of him.

Lando was being charged with conspiracy to distribute cocaine. The Denver police had received an anonymous tip that there was a deal going down at Lando's residence. Two kilos were found during their search. There was a lot going on around that case because Lando had claimed he was set up. That the drugs weren't his. That he would never bring drugs into his home.

"It might have been true. The detectives heard some talk around the streets that someone in Manetti's own organization had set Lando up. Somebody lower in the food chain that wanted to move up and was resentful of what they felt was special treatment for Lando. Whether the defense would have been able to build on that we never found out. The drugs went missing from the evidence locker. Without the drugs, we had no case. Right after that, a guy midway up in the Manetti organization disappeared. Might have been he left town. Might have been that Lando had been telling the truth and that this guy had something to do with setting him up, in which case he might have left on his own. Or, it could be he was helped in his disappearance. But there wasn't any missing person's report filed and nothing to warrant any further attention from the Denver police."

Ellie stopped talking and looked at Cord, waiting for him to ask her a follow-up question. She wasn't quite prepared, however, for the question he asked.

"And is it true that the suspicions centered around the handling of those two cases led to an internal investigation by the Denver District Attorney, eventually resulting in your being fired?"

It took every bit of Ellie's self-control not to shout out a denial to the question. She took a deep breath and held Cord's eyes.

"I have no knowledge of an internal investigation being conducted and I had no indication that the handling of the Manetti cases had anything to do with my being fired. It is true that Denver District Attorney Hanover and I had differing styles and frequently butted heads on what cases to prosecute and how to handle them. However, the two Manetti cases were not among those where there was a disagreement and I experienced no repercussions when the cases were dropped. In fact, I thought at the time it was odd that Hanover had not taken the opportunity to comment on my performance.

"Normally, our disagreements became moot as my win ratio was very high. So, on those occasions that I did lose at trial, Hanover almost always called me in to point out that I might have won if I had followed a different strategy, his strategy. He usually made a big show of putting a note in my personal file. Where did you get the idea that was the reason I was fired?"

"I'm sorry, Miss Nelson, that information is part of an ongoing case and I can't comment on that source. You've stated that you had no knowledge of an investigation and that you did not feel your handling of the Manetti cases resulted in your firing. Could you explain then why you were fired?"

Ellie paused for a few seconds and pulled the scene with Hanover into memory. She wanted to make sure she got it right.

"Insubordination, for starters."

"For starters?"

"Yes, that's what he said. He then added that I was lucky he wasn't charging me with tampering with evidence, at least not yet. As near as I can recall, those were his exact words. He then asked me to turn over a key chain I had in my possession as well as my laptop."

"Was the key chain the evidence in question?" Cord asked.

"Yes," replied Ellie. "I had obtained it from the police evidence locker the previous day. It was listed in the personal effects of Stephen Lindsey, a prominent Denver attorney."

"Why would having the key chain result in an accusation of insubordination?"

"The police had closed the case. There was a confession and the only thing left was the sentencing. I had some misgivings and wanted to pursue a couple of what I felt to be loose ends. When I petitioned Hanover to continue with my enquiries, he denied my request and ordered me, in no uncertain terms, to drop it."

Ellie went on to explain in more detail her hunch about Lindsey's key fob and that she just couldn't drop it. After she left the police building, she had driven to her apartment and copied the contents of the flash drive to her laptop. She had then gone out for a quick dinner and to attend her weekly art class. When she'd gotten back home, it was late and she had only had a chance to scan the information from the drive. Much of the information was written in what Ellie recognized as shorthand.

Although Ellie had taken a shorthand class, it had been many years ago and she was more than a bit rusty. So, she decided she would Google the shorthand alphabet when she got in the office the next day and make a full transcript of the file. She knew it was going to be a tedious exercise and had just been too tired to try to decipher the files that night.

At this point, Ellie stopped. "I need a break," she said.

Cord didn't protest and immediately said, "Recorder off."

CHAPTER 10

Ellie stood up from the table, walked to the refrigerator in the kitchen, and pulled out a bottle of iced tea. "Can I get anything for anyone else?" she asked. "I've got iced tea, lime soda, grape juice, and a few bottles of beer."

Ellie's dad jumped up from the table also and said, "You sit down, Princess, and start drinking your tea. I'll get the drinks."

Everyone opted for the tea also and no one seemed interested in a glass. So, Ellie's dad grabbed three more bottles from the refrigerator and brought them back to the table.

Cord smiled when he heard Howard Nelson call Ellie "Princess." It appeared that he wasn't the only one with a childhood nickname. As everyone twisted the cap off the bottle of tea and took a sip, Cord asked a question that he hoped would ease some of the tension that had built during Ellie's statement. He was anxious to finish the statement, but he needed a minute to process all the information Ellie had provided so far and to decide what he wanted to ask when he restarted the recorder.

"So, art lessons, huh?" Cord asked.

"Yes," Evelyn Nelson said as she jumped into the conversation, "I didn't know you were back into your art."

Ellie shot Cord a perturbed look. He didn't know why, but his question seemed to have generated more tension instead of easing it.

"You know painting has always been a stress reducer for me, Mother. The last couple of years have been particularly stressful. I knew I would never be able to break away from my work on my own, but, when I ran into a well-known artist at a charity event, I learned that she was offering classes.

"She accepted me as a student and it was perfect. The classes are one evening a week and cost enough that I would have felt wasteful if I missed even one class. I think painting is the one thing that has kept me sane."

Cord noted a look of displeasure on Evelyn Nelson's face and she started to speak. However, Howard Nelson reached over and gently laid his hand on his wife's arm. Although the words were unspoken, he was clearly telling his wife to let it go.

Ellie had also noted the interaction between her parents and was grateful for her father's intervention. Not wanting to chance it was short-lived, Ellie looked at Cord.

"I'd like to get this over with. Let's go on record again."

Cord reached over, turned on the recorder, and restated the names of those present. He then asked, "You mentioned you had read some of the files on the flash drive. Could you go into more detail?"

"As I recall, there were a dozen or so folders, with dates as filenames. The dates spanned the last couple of years. I opened two or three files and all appeared to contain multiple sheets of paper that had been scanned into the folders. I found it interesting that these were copies of handwritten notes using a combination of initials and shorthand."

"Do you recall any of the initials?"

"KC, R, and a D or D.A. or maybe both. JM and I think TM."

"And were you able to determine what the initials stood for?"

"Well, KC pretty much jumped out as Kansas City and I thought the D must be Denver. From the context in the notes, I really just made a leap that JM might stand for Jack Manetti. Probably because I've been involved in cases against him. I didn't really think at the time about the TM, but it seems obvious that if JM is Jack, then TM is Tommy. I didn't read enough at the time to get a feel for what the R stood for but I'm wondering now if it stood for Russo."

"What in the notes made you think that JM referred to Jack Manetti?" Cord asked.

"It might sound strange, but it was the way the notes were constructed," Ellie said as she pictured the files in her mind. "Other than being in shorthand, they reminded me of the way I make notes about cases I'm working on. I started looking at them from that perspective and began to pick out words like evidence, location, and meeting. Along with translating the shorthand, I had planned to search for cases that might have corresponded to the dates in the file names. But I didn't get that chance. I'm afraid I can't tell you much more."

"Just a couple more questions," Cord said. "Did you make any other copies of the files on the flash drive?"

"I wish I had, but I'm sorry to say that I did not. As far as I know there were only the original flash drive and the copy on my laptop."

"And you believe possession of the flash drive was the reason you were fired?"

"That's correct."

"Can you tell me why you believe that?"

"No, Special Agent Sinclair, I cannot. I'm still trying to understand it myself and anything I could say would be pure speculation. There's nothing more I can add."

Cord nodded and then spoke into the recorder. "Interview completed; recorder off," Cord said leaning back in his chair.

For a moment no one spoke. But then Cord stood up and broke the silence. "Ellie, I'm sure you have some questions and I know once I've had time to process everything, I'll want to talk with you again. But, right now, I need to send this recording to my team. We'll probably be working most of the night to determine how all this fits with our investigation."

Cord reached into a pocket, pulled out a business card, wrote a number on the back, and handed it to Ellie. "I'll get in touch with you tomorrow to set up a time to meet. If you need anything before that or think of anything else you feel might be helpful, my cell number is on the back."

Ellie didn't have a chance to do more than nod before her father stood and laid a hand on Cord's shoulder, guiding him toward the coat draped across the dining room chair. "You have to eat sometime," Howard Nelson said as he picked up the coat and held it open for Cord. Howard escorted Cord to the foyer and opened the front door. "We'll be going out to dinner later and you are welcome to join us. What do you think, Evelyn," he turned back toward his wife and asked, "Baxter's at 7?"

Without really waiting for an answer, Howard repeated the restaurant and time to Cord. "Baxter's at 7 p.m. Please join us if you can." With that, he ushered Cord as quickly out the door as he could.

CHAPTER 11

Evelyn gave her husband a confused look. "That was rather abrupt, Howard. What was the rush?"

"It's obvious that Ellie is just about spent. It was time for everyone to take a breather. And since it is also obvious that there is something going on between those two, I didn't want to take a chance that any procedural nonsense would put a damper on their relationship before it even gets started."

"You've always been a romantic, Howard. But I have to agree. I can't wait to get in touch with Catherine."

"Hey! I'm right here!" Ellie said to her parents. "And there is no relationship."

Ellie hadn't said a word since Cord had stopped the recording. It was true she felt drained and she just didn't have the energy to do more than watch as her father had walked Cord to the door. She had been sitting in a daze, staring into space, until her parents' words started to register. Relationship? What relationship? As she protested there was no relationship, Ellie knew her parents didn't believe her. And why should they? She didn't believe it herself. No, there was definitely something there and it was something she definitely wanted to pursue. Ellie decided it was best not to focus on that subject and picked up on the other observation her dad had made.

"You're right, Dad. I'm really dragging. I think I could use a shower and a nap before we go out for dinner." She turned to walk down the hallway toward her bedroom, but stopped almost immediately and turned back toward her parents.

"Thanks, Dad. Thanks, Mom. I'm glad you were here," she said softly and stepped quickly forward, giving each of them a kiss on the cheek. She turned back again and went into her bedroom, closing the door behind her.

Ellie looked down at her feet and couldn't believe she still had on the Ulu boots she had laced up and worn outside earlier that morning. Was that just this morning? She sat on the edge of her bed and, as she unlaced the boots, she began to replay the day's events in her mind.

The next thing she knew she awoke to a dark room and voices out in the hall. She didn't remember lying back on the bed after taking off her boots; but she could see by the clock on her nightstand that she'd been asleep for over 3 hours. It was 6 p.m. and she needed to hustle to take a shower and get ready to go out for dinner.

There was a light rap on her bedroom door. Ellie walked over to the door and opened it to see her mother standing there, looking fantastic in a cowl-necked cashmere sweater and wool slacks.

"Sorry, Mom, I was really out. I'll be ready in a half hour."

Ellie shut the door, raced across the room to her en suite bathroom, peeling off clothes as she went. She stepped into the shower and as the warm jets of water hit her, she would have loved to stay there for about an hour. Instead she quickly showered and washed her hair. As she stepped out of the shower, she wrapped a towel around her head and wrapped herself in the terry cloth robe that had been hanging on the back of the bathroom door.

Ellie went into the walk-in closet and using what her mother had been wearing as a guide, picked out a hunter green turtleneck sweater and a pair of Pendleton black watch plaid slacks. She also pulled out the pair of Cole Hahn booties that she had been wearing when she'd left Denver in such a hurry. They were her favorite winter shoe. They were a classic style that went with almost anything. The added bonus was that they had a low heel and were waterproof.

Ellie dressed quickly and went back in to her bathroom to do something with her hair and makeup. This was one of those times that Ellie was glad of her natural curls. She just finger combed her hair as she moved the blow dryer around her head. Once dry, she spritzed on some styling spray and shaped a few strands of hair around her face. A touch of mascara, blush and lip gloss and she decided that was as good as she was going to get if they were going to make their 7 o'clock reservation.

Her guess that she might be cutting it close was confirmed when she walked out her bedroom and almost bumped into her mother who was standing right outside her door.

"Your father is already in the car waiting for us," Evelyn said as she handed Ellie her coat, purse and cell phone. Ellie shrugged into her coat and followed after her mother toward the garage.

It didn't take long to arrive at the restaurant. The roads were free of snow as was Baxter's parking lot. Although the lot was nearly full, a car had just exited a spot directly in front of the restaurant's walkway.

"Ha!" Howard said, as he quickly turned into the spot. "We'll look at this as a good omen!"

Like many of the homes and businesses in the Lake of the Ozarks, placement of the structures and access to those structures was often interesting due to the hilly terrain that surrounded the lake itself. In the case of Baxter's, its parking lot was several feet lower than street level, and the restaurant itself was several feet lower than the parking lot. This meant that they walked down about 10 steps before they reached the entry courtyard and the doors to the restaurant.

Although the snow had been cleared and the stairs were well lit, Ellie would have been a little tentative had she not worn her low-heeled boots. When they'd made their way down the stairs and entered the restaurant, there was a flurry of activity as they were greeted by a receptionist who confirmed their reservation and checked their coats. Howard indicated one other person would possibly be joining them and they were then escorted by a hostess to a table for four with a magnificent view of The Lake.

Two sides of the dining room were floor to ceiling windows that took on the dark colors of the night sky. Rather than being eerie, it gave the dining room a warm, cozy feel and was the perfect palette for capturing The Lake's nighttime beauty. As you looked out the windows, the lights from the houses along the shoreline and the blue lights dotting the boat docks, created a shimmering dance in the rippling water.

"Wow," said Ellie as she sat in one of the chairs next to the windows. "This is absolutely beautiful."

"It's become a real favorite of ours," Evelyn said. "As you've noticed, the view is one of the best you will find at The Lake and the food is exceptional."

"It's just now seven," Howard said. "Let's order our drinks and then wait a few minutes to see if Cord joins us before ordering anything else."

The waiter had appeared and taken their drink orders. Ellie and her mother had ordered a glass of wine and, as the designated driver, Ellie's father had ordered a seltzer and lime.

A few minutes later Ellie saw the waiter coming toward their table with a tray of drinks. He was followed closely by the hostess who was leading Cord toward their table. Ellie studied him as he walked through the restaurant. He looked somewhat harried as he scanned the restaurant. His eyes found Ellie's and he waved off the hostess, stepped around the waiter and hurried to their table.

"Ellie, we need to talk."

Before anything else could be said, the waiter arrived at the table and began to distribute the drinks. He looked at Cord, who was still standing beside the table.

"Will you be staying, Sir? Can I take your coat and get you something to drink?"

"No, I won't be..."

Howard Nelson interrupted, "Nonsense, Cord. I'd bet you haven't eaten anything since we last saw you. That means that, like all of us, you are famished. Anything you have to say, can wait until after we've eaten."

Cord obviously knew when he was beaten. He shrugged out of his coat and handed it to the waiter. With a quick glance at the table, he pointed to Howard's glass and said, "I'll have what he's having."

Other than agreeing that they were going to skip the appetizers and go directly for the entrees, there was no other conversation until the waiter returned with Cord's drink and they gave him their orders. Ellie smiled because her mother and Cord had both gone with the lighter fish specialties, while she and her father ordered thick ribeye steaks.

Ellie's father monopolized the conversation throughout dinner, talking about his Porsche, the weather and anything else besides the events of the day. As they were all finishing up their meal, Evelyn spoke.

"Cord, I know you want to talk with Ellie but this probably isn't the place to do it. Howard, when you see the waiter, let him know that you'd like the check and two slices of their gooey butter cake and two fudge brownies packaged to go. We'll have dessert and coffee back at the house and Cord can tell us all what he's learned."

There was no chance for anyone to object or make another suggestion. The waiter had appeared and Howard had followed Evelyn's instructions. After the check had been paid and the bags with the desserts had arrived, they all stood, retrieved their coats from the hostess and left the restaurant.

As they climbed the stairs to the parking lot Cord said, "Ellie, why don't you ride with me?"

Ellie had been quiet most of the evening. Cord had taken the open seat next to her at the restaurant. She had been fully aware of him next to her and had stolen side glances at him frequently throughout the meal. She couldn't deny how attracted she was to him, but she wasn't ready yet to do anything about it. There was too much going on at the moment.

"Maybe it's best if I ride back with my folks. We all want to hear what you have to say and you might as well only say it once."

Cord looked like he was going to say something but must have decided against it. As Howard pressed the alarm to unlock the car and moved around the passenger side to open the door for Evelyn, Cord opened the door for Ellie and said he would see them at the house. Ellie watched as he braced against the chill of the night and walked toward the far end of the lot. He obviously hadn't had Howard's good fortune in finding a parking spot.

CHAPTER 12

Back at the house, Ellie had quickly made a pot of coffee while her mother set out the desserts, plates, napkins, knives, forks and spoons on the dining room table. Ellie's dad was hanging up the coats and, hearing steps on the porch, he pulled open the door before Cord could knock.

"I'll take your coat. Go on over to the dining room. We won't delay this any longer."

"Help yourselves to the desserts," Evelyn said as she placed four mugs, sugar cubes and a creamer on the table. "It will be just a minute for the coffee, but I'll bring it over as soon as it's ready. Go ahead and start if you want, Cord, I can hear fine from the kitchen."

"First," Cord said, as he transferred a piece of one of the fudge brownies to his plate, "I want to thank you for dinner. Baxter's is one of my favorite places to eat when I am down in this area and I couldn't have asked for better company. I hope we'll all be able to do this again under different circumstances and, next time, it's my treat."

As Ellie's mother brought the coffee to the table and poured some in each of the mugs, Cord got to what they all wanted to hear.

"I've been on the phone for several hours working various pieces of information Ellie gave us in her interview. One of the first things we looked into was a connection between Stephen Lindsey and the Manetti's. We didn't find one other than Ellie as a common link. But not liking the coincidence that there were two lawyers who died within days of each other, both falling from a parking garage, we decided to see if we could find a connection between the two lawyers.

"Bingo! We discovered that Lindsey and Carter had attended law school together in Kansas City. Later tonight, we'll be working to finalize what needs to be done tomorrow. We'll need to look into the Carter and Lindsey investigations. I suspect we will all have to tread lightly with the D.A.'s office in Denver but we're going to want your laptop, the flash drive and any files pertaining to the cases you worked against Jack Manetti. Right now, it is only your word that those files exist and that there was a tie between Stephen Lindsey and the Manetti's. We're hoping to get new information that will shed some light on any communications between the two lawyers and what if anything might have led to their deaths. Carter's death was always suspicious and it's looking like it needs to be revisited. As I said, Lindsey's murder is just too much of a coincidence."

Cord had paused to take a sip of his coffee. Ellie figured he had covered most everything and had a forkful of gooey butter cake half way to her mouth when Cord dropped the real bombshell that caused Ellie to drop her fork and her parents to stare back and forth between Cord and Ellie in alarm.

"And although I don't have proof, I'm convinced you're in danger, Ellie. I believe that gunshot this morning was meant for you."

"What?" Ellie and her parents exclaimed in unison.

Cord explained they had surveillance on Manetti in Kansas City and one of the task force members remembered seeing something about The Ozarks in one of the transcripts.

"About three days ago Tommy Manetti was overheard talking to someone about finding a package he'd lost. He said he'd found it at the Lake of the Ozarks and asked the person on the other end of the phone to take care of it. I believe it took them a couple of days to find you after you left Denver."

"But it was a man that was shot, not Ellie," Howard said.

"My yellow jacket," said Ellie softly.

"Yes, Ellie, your yellow jacket," Cord said in an equally soft tone as he looked over at Ellie with obvious concern. He held her eyes and then continued to explain.

"Ellie, you told the Sheriff's deputy that you had been jogging early mornings and that the murder victim had accidently or purposely run into you along your route and tried to start up a conversation. In his last attempt, he mentioned that he had a yellow jacket just like the one you were wearing.

"That's why I left you during your interview with the deputy. I hadn't taken a good look at the victim this morning and I wanted to play out a hunch. I drove to the hospital and met up with the county Medical Examiner Investigator who was prepping the body for transport to Nixa, Missouri, for an autopsy. The investigator allowed me to look at the yellow jacket the victim had been wearing and confirmed his height, weight and overall body statistics.

"The information was right along the lines of what I had been thinking. The victim was approximately the same height as Ellie, was very slender and was wearing a yellow jacket just like one that Ellie has."

Cord went on to explain that when he returned to speak with Ellie, he had outlined his thoughts to the Sheriff and while still uneasy was somewhat pacified by the Sheriff's comments that there were hundreds of jackets like that at The Lake and that the victim had been a very unpopular man.

But, after the interview with Ellie and the subsequent information learned by the task force, Cord was now convinced Ellie had been the intended target.

"I'm afraid that once the news about a Lake Ozark alderman being shot hits the papers tomorrow,

Manetti will find out his shooter hit the wrong person and there will likely be another attempt made on Ellie. We don't have enough right now to arrange protective custody, but I don't think it's a good idea for Ellie to stay here, especially by herself." Cord said that last part, taking his eyes off Ellie and looking at her parents in turn.

"I agree," Howard said immediately. "We can leave in the morning and Ellie can come back to Kansas City with us. While it is not a fortress by any means, we do have a gated entrance and a good security system. We also have some weapons in the house and we are all certified and fully capable of using those weapons if necessary."

Ellie thought for just a moment about objecting. She didn't like other people making decisions for her. But she had to admit that it made sense to take some precautions. There was nothing really keeping her at The Lake for the time being and it would be good to be closer to where Cord would be. "Wait a minute, where had that thought come from?" Ellie thought to herself.

Everyone was looking at her when she finally spoke, "Sounds like a plan," she said, "on the condition that you keep me up to date on what is happening."

"You know there are some things I can't share, but I'll tell you what I can."

"Deal," Ellie said quickly.

With that, everyone stood up and Ellie walked around the table to escort Cord to the door.

"You have my card. Please call me once you are settled at your parents' house."

There was an awkward moment where Ellie wanted to say something to keep Cord from leaving but not knowing what to say she just laid her hand on his arm.

"Thank you, Cord," she said softly.

Cord gave her a look that warmed her to her core. She saw genuine concern and maybe something more as he simply nodded and then turned and walked down the steps and toward the driveway.

Ellie was letting cold air into the house. So, she shut the door and went into the living room where her parents were standing in full view of the front door and the exchange between her and Cord. She ignored the look they were giving her; she wasn't going to get into a discussion about Cord.

"I hope this all turns out to be nothing and that I haven't gotten you involved in my mess."

"Whatever it turns out to be, we are involved and will stay that way," Ellie's mom asserted in her most officious tone. Then she smiled mischievously and said, "And I can't wait to call Catherine when we get home."

Part 2 – Kansas City

CHAPTER 13

Early the next morning, they closed up The Lake house and drove back to Kansas City. During the three-hour trip, Ellie brought her parents up to date on the two cases she had prosecuted against Jack Manetti and the details about the Stephen Lindsey murder.

As she had anticipated, her mother was interested in the details of the cases. Although Ellie really valued her mother as a sounding board, she had an ulterior motive. If she kept her mother focused on the cases, then no one would bring up the elephant or, in this case, elephants plural, in the room...um car. First there was the whole Cord thing and the possibilities of a relationship. Second there was the issue of what Ellie planned to do since she was out of a job. She had no answer for those two things, but it was the third topic that Ellie wanted to avoid the most. Eventually, her mother would want to discuss the art classes.

Ellie's great-grandmother, Euzenia Nelson, had given her a set of paints when she was seven years old. Her Grandma Zenie, as she called her, had been a student of Thomas Hart Benton during his time at the Kansas City Art Institute. While she had not reached the fame of her teacher or some of his other students, her great-grandmother was very passionate about her art, and she had passed that passion on to Ellie. Over a five-year period, Ellie had spent many hours painting and listening to her Grandma Zenie tell stories about famous artists.

Even after her great-grandmother's death, Ellie had continued her love of art. Through Middle and High School, she had taken whatever art classes were available and had excelled in them. She had been told that she had a real talent. Her art teacher felt she could have her choice of any university with a Fine Arts Program.

The problem was that it had always been expected Ellie would follow her mother into a law career. Ellie had been a straight-A student and she could also have her choice of Law Schools. After a discussion with her parents about career opportunities and potential earnings from a law degree versus one in fine arts, Ellie had agreed that pursuing a law program was the better way to go.

The demands of university classes and summer internships meant that Ellie had little time to paint, and by the time she had started her career in the Denver D.A.'s office, her easel and paints were seldom brought out of storage. The classes she had recently started taking had shown Ellie just how much she had missed her painting. She realized there had actually been a major void in her life that was no longer there now that she was painting again.

Ellie was brought out of her thoughts when she realized they had stopped and were at the gates of her childhood home. Just as Ellie's dad punched in a code and the gates began to swing open, Ellie's phone signaled she had received an Instagram. It was from her friend Lisa and showed a brief video of Denver's F.B.I. Special Agent in Charge being escorted by Hanover back toward his office. "OMG," read the accompanying text. "Do you know what this is about? Call me tonight."

After Ellie's dad drove the car into the garage and stopped, both parents turned and looked at Ellie in the backseat. She queued up the video and held up her phone so both her parents could see it and explained who the two men were in the video.

"I'll call Lisa later and find out what the office grapevine has to say. Right now, I'm going to call Cord to let him know we got here. It will probably go to voicemail since I'm guessing he is busy with the investigations he was trying to coordinate here in Kansas City."

"Why don't you invite him here for dinner or coffee later; we'll order something to be delivered. Maybe you'll be able to get him to fill you in on what happened today," Ellie's mom suggested.

They entered the house through the mudroom that connected the garage to the kitchen. Nostalgia immediately overtook Ellie as she reached the breakfast nook. She hadn't been home for a couple of years and she was immediately flooded with memories of sitting at the nook's table doing homework, eating snacks, or playing board games. Her parents, on the other hand, had walked right through the kitchen heading, Ellie was sure, to their respective offices. Ellie felt a bit guilty that her troubles had caused her parents to shuffle their schedules. She knew her mother was always involved in multiple cases and her father was preparing for an annual meeting. They most likely had a lot to catch up on.

"You know where to find us if you need us, Princess."

"The maid service was here last week; so, your room should be fine, Eleanor."

Ellie was now alone in the kitchen. She went to the refrigerator and pulled out a bottled water. She sat down at the table in the breakfast nook and pulled Cord's business card out of her purse. She first recorded the number on the back of the card into her phone's contacts and then pushed the icon to make a call.

As she suspected it would, the call went to voicemail. She left a brief message that they had arrived in Kansas City and then extended the invitation for dinner or coffee if he had the time later. She added that she was wondering if his team had been successful in finding the information they had planned to go after that day. She made no mention of the fact that she already knew about the events in Denver.

Ellie was not usually one to sit idle and she realized she had been wasting time at the Lake of the Ozarks, mostly sitting and feeling sorry for herself. Sure, she had been trying to make sense of her firing, and what she was going to do with her life, but she hadn't really delved too deep.

With the new information that she had learned, she believed now, more than ever, there was more to Stephen Lindsey's murder than was originally thought. She went over to the desk in the kitchen and pulled out a pen and legal pad. There was never a shortage of legal pads around the house. Her father and especially her mother used them for everything from a simple to do list to notes for a business plan or legal strategy.

She sat back at the table and started making some notes. There was an obvious connection from Lindsey in Denver to Rob Carter in Kansas City. Carter, in turn, was connected to Gino Russo who was replaced by Tommy Manetti. Tommy Manetti was the brother of Jack Manetti, which brought her full circle back to Denver. Her hunch about Lindsey's bullet key chain had led to a series of events that didn't appear to be over.

Next, she made three columns. One each for Gino Russo, Rob Carter and Stephen Lindsey. She drew an arrow between Rob Carter and Lindsey and on the arrow's line she wrote "law school". Under Gino Russo, she noted his death and Tommy Manetti replacing him as head of what was suspected to be an organized crime syndicate in Kansas City. Under Rob Carter, who had been Gino Russo's attorney, she listed his suicide. She included several entries under Lindsey showing his murder and Hanover telling her to let the case go. Next, she wrote her own name, noting the flash drive and copy to her laptop, followed by Hanover confiscating both items and firing her. She listed herself again, noting Nelson at The Lake. Finally, she wrote "Doug Withers murdered – TARGET?"

Ellie sat back and stared at the notes on the legal pad to see if she missed anything. It certainly covered the current events. But as she thought about it, she suspected the Jack Manetti cases she had prosecuted back in Denver were a part of all this. She was convinced at this point that Hanover was in bed with Jack Manetti and that she had been determined to be a threat. She added Jack Manetti's name in the first column and drew an arrow from the entry for

Hanover confiscating her laptop over to Manetti's name. She listed Tommy Manetti again under Jack and added "Unknown Shooter" in the middle column between Manetti's name in the first column and the murder of Doug Withers in the last column. It was rather convoluted and there were definitely some missing pieces, but Ellie was convinced that she had the events and their sequence correct for what she suspected at that point in time.

The longer Ellie sat there and looked at the notes she'd made, the madder she got. Sure, she had agreed to come back to Kansas City, but she had no intention of hiding behind the gates of her parents' home. She had some ideas to pursue, but she first had some shopping to do.

She found her father in his den. It was probably just as you would imagine the den of a respected banker to look like. It had mahogany bookcases that lined one wall and were the same rich color as the massive desk that dominated the room. Two red leather wing back chairs sat facing the desk. The door to the den was open and Ellie could see her father sitting in his chair with his back to the door. He was looking out the window behind his desk that had a view of the landscaped backyard. Ellie rapped lightly on the door as she entered. Her father swiveled around at the sound of her knock. He was holding a phone in one hand and with the other held up one finger indicating that he would be just a minute.

Ellie sat in one of the wing back chairs and waited for her father to finish his call. She studied the rest of the office. She smiled at the massive globe standing in one corner of the room. Ellie knew that some decorator had originally designed the room. Her father actually preferred more modern styles, but he had admitted that unless he wanted to take out the walls and bookcases, the traditional design suited the room. Over the years, he had simply grown comfortable with the room and although he had added a few new items, it remained unchanged for the most part, right down to the green shade lamp on one corner of his desk.

Her father finished his call and looked across his desk at Ellie. "How are you doing, Princess?"

"I'm fine, Dad. I was just wondering if I could borrow one of the cars. I've got some things I need to pick up and thought I'd go down to the Plaza."

"Do you think that's wise? Shouldn't you just stay put?

Ellie knew her dad was concerned and so was she. But, if she was in danger, she didn't think there was any way she would have a problem this soon. And that's what she convinced her dad of as well. She had no intention of letting him know she was going to make a few detours while she was out.

"Here are the keys to the Cayenne," Ellie's dad said. "You can just keep those and feel free to use the car whenever you want while you're here. Oh, and you might need this," he said as he wrote something on a piece of paper and handed it to Ellie.

Ellie smiled as she looked at the numbers on the paper and recognized them as the month and date of her parents' anniversary. She wouldn't need the paper and handed it back to her dad.

"You are just an incurable romantic, Dad."

"I'm afraid not, Princess. Your mother reset the code when I forgot our anniversary last month. She said that maybe if I had to punch it in every day, I wouldn't forget next year."

Ellie thanked her dad and she was still chuckling when she left his den and made a quick trip upstairs to her bedroom. As her mother had said, the room looked perfect and was the same as Ellie had left it when she had moved to Denver. Like her dad, she had never had a desire to change the design of her room and her mother had not changed it after she left. She'd always loved the room. It was very feminine without being juvenile. She took in the white, four-poster bed that was the focal point of the room. The duvet and pillow shams had a delicate rose pattern that was repeated in the drapes that framed the windows in the room. The walls were painted a dusty rose and several accent rugs were placed around the room softening the effect of the dark hardwood floor. Matching white night stands, a dresser, desk and chair completed the furniture in the room. There was a connecting bathroom and a large walk-in closet which was where she headed now.

Ellie did a quick survey of the closet. She'd always kept some clothes here for the times she would visit. It was much easier than carrying suitcases back and forth. Although there was nothing wrong with the clothes she saw, her tastes had changed in the couple of years that had passed since her last visit. She could think of a few things she would want to have while she was in Kansas City. Eventually, she was going to need to do something about her condo and her things in Denver. She hadn't spoken of it to anyone yet, but she knew that she was not going to stay in Denver when all this was over. But those thoughts had to go on the back burner for the moment.

CHAPTER 14

Ellie had to agree with her dad's enthusiasm for the Cayenne. The car had every luxury imaginable and really did make her feel secure behind the wheel. It handled beautifully and she could almost feel the power that was there if she chose to use it. It was a far different car than her Prius. She liked the Prius and as with most people who owned one, she felt somewhat smug for her small part in helping the environment. But after only a few minutes behind the wheel of the Cayenne, she thought the Prius might end up another casualty of the changes she would need to make.

Ellie drove down Wornall Road toward the Country Club Plaza. The drive was filled with memories since she had grown up in the area. First, she passed Loose Park where she remembered an epic egg fight that had taken place one moonlit night between the boys and girls in her senior class. They were having a great time until they heard sirens, scrambled to their cars and drove out of the park as fast as they could. It was a close call but the police didn't catch anyone. Ellie and several other girls had driven together and ended up at the house of one of the girls for an impromptu slumber party. Most of the remaining night consisted of washing egg out of their hair and swapping stories about which boys they had splattered. Next, she drove by the lower campus of Pembroke Hill Academy where she had attended elementary school. As she crossed the bridge over Brush Creek into the Country Club Plaza area, she thought about what shops she could hit. She took a left on Nichols and her decision was made for her. There was an open parking spot right in front of the Eddie Bauer store.

A quick look and she also spotted a Victoria's Secret across the street. Between those two stores, Ellie figured she could get all the things she needed to augment her wardrobe. She parked the car and dashed into Eddie Bauer. It didn't take her long to find a pair of leggings, some flannel lined jeans, a flannel shirt, a cable knit sweater, and a couple of long-sleeved T's. She was headed toward the checkout when she walked by a section of shoes and she was immediately in love. A pair of butterscotch-colored leather hiking boots caught her eye and she decided she just had to have them. She picked them up and couldn't believe how soft the leather felt and they were much lighter than the hiking boots she had left back home. She found her size and took everything to the register. She was confident everything would fit and didn't bother trying anything on.

When she left Eddie Bauer, she transferred her bags into the back of the Cayenne, locked it back up and then did another quick jog to the end of the block and across the street to Victoria's Secret. She knew exactly what she wanted, made a quick purchase and was out of the store and heading back to her parking spot in under fifteen minutes. She was almost to the SUV when a jacket in the window of Free People caught her eye. It was a fluffy dolman style jacket with a hood. Ellie hadn't shopped at Free People before as the clothes they carried were not the type of thing Ellie normally wore. But she seemed to be going outside the box a lot lately. On an impulse, she went inside the store and bought the jacket, which she thought would look great with her leggings.

Ellie opened the SUV, threw the remaining packages into the back and then climbed into the driver's seat. She was not sure where exactly she needed to go for her next stop. She really needed to get a laptop to replace the one that Hanover had confiscated back in Denver. Between her cell phone and the laptop that technically belonged to the D.A.'s office, Ellie had never found a need for another device. She needed one now. One she could use to capture her notes and research all the players in this whole mess.

It dawned on Ellie that the Cayenne was probably equipped with a voice navigation system. Most systems allowed you to find nearby stores, restaurants, hotels, etc. Ellie punched the button for the voice system and said, "Computer Store." The navigation screen displayed a map with a dot that indicated a store was located about two blocks directly behind where she was now parked. Ellie laughed when she saw that it was an Apple store. Once again, it seemed she was being led in a direction she would not normally take. She had never used a Mac before but she knew it would have the basic functions she needed. The important thing was that she get something quickly. She had a feeling that things were going to be moving fast and she wanted to be one step ahead.

Ellie pulled out of her parking spot and drove around the block, turning right on Nichols this time to go in the other direction. Once again, luck was with her and she found a parking spot right in front of the Apple Store. She was immediately greeted by a salesperson who she told she was looking for a laptop. That brought a thin smile from the salesperson who obviously didn't have the term laptop in his lexicon. He began talking about the various iPads and MacBooks and led Ellie to the area of the store where several different models were on display. She had the salesperson give her a demonstration of how to access the browser and word processing program from each of the machines and quickly settled on the new MacBook which only weighed 2 lbs. and would fit in her purse. She left the store with the MacBook, a protective sleeve and wireless earphones. Ellie had added so much to her credit card in the last couple of hours that she was surprised she hadn't gotten a call from the card company to verify it was her making the purchases.

Finally satisfied that she had everything she needed, Ellie drove back to the house. She punched in the code at the gate and then pressed the button on the visor that would open the garage door. As she pulled into the garage, she noticed neither her father's Porsche nor her mother's Mercedes were there. She had no doubt they had both driven into their respective offices to get in a few hours of work. Ellie was proven correct when she walked into the breakfast nook and saw a note to that effect propped up on the table. It also said that her mother was going to pick up Chinese food on the way back home and dinner would be at 6:30. That gave Ellie a couple of hours to herself and she was going to make good use of it. She was turning to walk out of the kitchen when it registered with her that there was a newspaper sitting on the table. It was that day's Kansas City Star. It was opened to a section that contained regional news, and in the lower right had corner, there was an article circled. The title read "Lake Ozark Alderman Murdered." The article mentioned that Doug Withers had been found in a residential area, dead from a gunshot wound. It went on to say that Withers had voted for several controversial local developments and the Sheriff was pursuing all leads. It then advised that anyone having information about the shooting should call the Camden County Sheriff's office.

She thought about the ramifications of the article as she took all the packages up to her bedroom. She put away all her clothes and then began setting up the MacBook on her desk. The setup was very straightforward and she was connected and online in just a few minutes. She thought the first thing she would do was get an online subscription to the Kansas City and Denver newspapers. She would start with the Kansas City paper. She wanted to find the articles leading up to and immediately following the deaths of Gino Russo and his attorney, Rob Carter.

Ellie had just brought up the subscription page to the Kansas City Star when her cell phone rang. She pulled the phone out of her purse and looked at the display.

"Hey, Lisa. Are you okay?"

"Wow, when you texted me last night and said I'd want to be sure and be at work today, I never would have guessed the F.B.I. would show up. Did you see the video I sent this morning? I'm assuming you know what is going on."

"I do know some of it. How about you tell me about this morning and then I'll fill you in on what I know."

Lisa proceeded to tell Ellie how the F.B.I.'s S.A.C. had appeared in the reception area with two other agents. Apparently, they had an appointment, because Carla, the receptionist, immediately buzzed Hanover who came to the front desk and personally escorted the three men into the conference room. A few minutes later, Hanover had called his secretary, Virginia, and Paul Denton into the conference. Paul was the Chief Deputy D.A. and part of his function was to make case assignments. He came out of the conference room and went through the maze of cubicles, asking several of the staff to go into the conference room. Lisa was one of those people.

Lisa had entered the conference room and taken one of the chairs and waited as Jerry, another of the paralegals, Teri, a Victim's Advocate, and Carson, an investigator, all entered and took a seat at the table.

When everyone was seated, Hanover advised them that the Denver F.B.I. team was participating in a joint task force with the F.B.I.'s Kansas City office regarding potential violations of the RICO act by John and Thomas Manetti. Although they knew the cases had not gone to trial, they wanted to review the files to see if there was information that might be helpful for their current investigation. Hanover went on to add that the F.B.I. had received a tip that the recently deceased Stephen Lindsey might have had a tie to the Manetti's. Finally, Hanover looked at each of the people in the room and said they had all been called in because they had worked on the cases involving Jack Manetti or Stephen Lindsey and that he had already informed the agents that, although Eleanor Nelson had been the prosecutor assigned to the cases, she was no longer with the D.A.'s office. He encouraged each of the D.A. staff members to cooperate fully with the agents. But he added if they felt unsure about what should be provided or felt any evidence would be compromised, they should see either himself or Paul Denton.

With that, the F.B.I. agents took over and asked each of the staff members to begin accessing the appropriate files and they would call them into the conference room to discuss the files and their individual knowledge of the cases.

Since Lisa had always been the primary paralegal supporting Ellie, she knew where to access the files Ellie had stored in the central case database, as well as her own. The rest of the day had been spent going through folders and copying files onto flash drives the agents had provided. She only took a couple of breaks to go to the restroom and to grab a sandwich from the food truck that parked out on the side of the building during the lunch hour. As she came back from lunch, she saw Matt, one of the guys from the IT group, handing a laptop to Carla at the reception desk. He told Carla she was supposed to give it to Hanover's secretary, Virginia.

Toward the end of the day, Lisa was called into a vacant office where she handed a flash drive containing her files to the agent. She'd been interviewed for about an hour. Along with questions about the cases she had worked, they had also asked her questions about her relationship with Ellie and her opinion on how Ellie had handled the cases. They also asked her to recount the day Ellie was fired. In particular, they wanted to know if she had been aware that the key chain was a flash drive and if she had any knowledge as to the contents of the flash drive Ellie had obtained from the Denver Police Department and handed over to the D.A. on that day.

Lisa finally wound down her description.

"So, what's up, Ellie?"

"I don't know all of it," Ellie said. "But I can make some guesses and hopefully I'll learn more from Cord this evening. But, from what you've just described, I'm guessing the laptop you saw Matt carrying was probably mine. If Matt had it, then I'm assuming it was in IT's queue to wipe clean and format for a new user. If that had already been done, it is not going to be of any use. Since Teri was the Victim's Advocate for Stephen Lindsey's family, she would have been the one to return the key chain to the family. That is if Hanover followed through with his comment. It's been over a week now and, no matter what, the chain of custody has been broken. So, I'm not sure what help that will be if the Lindsey family still has it. But it must have something on it if someone is targeting me just because I might have read the files on it."

"What?" cried Lisa. "Targeting you how?"

"Oh, I guess I haven't had a chance to tell you that part. We're pretty much in agreement here that the bullet that killed the alderman down at The Lake was actually meant for me."

"Wow! I don't like the sound of that at all, Ellie. How can you sound so casual about it?"

"Well, for one thing, we're not positive. So, you can't say anything to anyone. I hope to hear more when I talk with Cord later."

Right then, Ellie's phone vibrated indicating she had another call. "Speak of the devil, Lisa; Cord is on the other line. I'll call you tomorrow when I know more."

Ellie disconnected with Lisa and swiped the icon to take the call from Cord.

"Hi, Cord. Any news?"

"A lot has happened today and I can tell you some of it. I'd rather not get into it on the phone. Is the offer for dinner still good?"

Ellie assured him that it was and asked if he needed directions to the house. He said he already had the address plugged into his GPS and would see them all in about a half hour.

By P. L. Gertner

CHAPTER 15

Ellie gave up on doing any research. She changed quickly into her new pair of leggings, the oversized cable knit sweater that went down half way to her knees, and slipped her feet into a pair of Ugg slides she had spotted in her closet earlier. She fluffed out her hair and added a bit of lip gloss and decided that would have to do. Downstairs in the kitchen, Ellie began transferring glasses, plates, silverware, and napkins to the breakfast nook table. She wasn't sure if her mother would have preferred to use the formal dining room, but this seemed like a more comfortable place to share the take-out and get the latest developments from Cord.

Ellie heard the door from the garage open and rushed through the mudroom to take some of the packages her mother was carrying into the house.

"Your father and Cord are right behind me. If you'll start setting out the food, I'll go drop my things in my office and be back in just a few minutes."

Sure enough, Ellie's father entered through the mudroom with Cord following close on his heels.

"Let me take your coat, Cord," Howard Nelson said. "You just have a seat."

That left Ellie and Cord standing alone in the kitchen and they just stared awkwardly at each other for a moment. Ellie had an urge to close the gap between them. It had been a hectic day and she hadn't realized until that moment that she had been stressed to the maximum. As her eyes held Cord's, she could feel the tension leaving and there was nothing she would have liked better than to feel Cord's arms around her. She thought she could see the same feelings in Cord's eyes but with the blink of an eye, she saw a flash of what looked like sadness or resignation and then Cord broke the eye contact and glanced around the kitchen.

"Is there anything I can help with?"

Ellie tried not to let her disappointment show and wondered what that was all about. Maybe she had been wrong. She thought there was something growing between them. But now she wasn't sure. She straightened her shoulders and put on a smile.

"How about you start pulling containers out of those bags and setting them in the middle of the table? What would you like to drink? I'm going to have a beer. But we've also got wine, water, soft drinks, or I can make coffee or tea."

"I've had enough coffee to float a battleship. A beer would be great."

Ellie's parents both came into the kitchen and decided they, too, would have a beer. Ellie grabbed four bottles and passed them around as she came back to the table. The next several minutes were taken up with the four of them opening containers and passing them around so that each could fill their plates. It looked like Ellie's mother had bought one of everything. Lemon chicken, sweet and sour pork, beef with broccoli, shrimp in lobster sauce, vegetables, fried rice, steamed rice, lo mein and egg rolls.

Cord speared a piece of broccoli and had just begun to chew, when Evelyn looked at him and said,

"So, I had a nice conversation with your mother earlier. She tells me you're engaged. Have you and your fiancée set a date?"

Cord's eyes got big and it looked like he used considerable control not to spit out what was in his mouth. He choked slightly and Howard reached over and gave him a sharp pat on the back.

Ellie glanced quickly at her mother who had a rather sly look on her face. She knew that look. It was one she had seen in the courtroom when her mother had asked a question for a particular effect, and to set up a witness for a later series of questions. She wondered just what else her mother had learned from Catherine Sinclair.

They were all watching Cord, waiting for him to answer the question.

Ellie caught a quick glimpse of the same sadness or resignation she had seen in Cord's eyes just a few minutes earlier.

"Uh, yes," Cord started as he began to regain his composure. "I am engaged. But, no, Charlotte and I have not set a date. The task force has been taking up most of my time and Charlotte has been so busy with her work in Boston that we haven't had a chance to talk about it much."

"Yes, long distance relationships can be very difficult," Evelyn said smoothly.

Cord just gave a brief nod and it was obvious he was not going to elaborate further. Ellie decided to give him a break and spoke before her mother could ask more about his fiancée.

"Cord, can you tell us what has happened today? Were you able to get either my laptop or the flash drive from the Denver D.A.? And do we know yet if I'm in danger?"

Cord seemed relieved at the change of subject and, between bites, began to fill them in on the day's events.

"Our Denver S.A.C. made an appointment and he and a couple of our agents went to the D.A.'s office this morning. Mitchell Hanover was already aware of the task force focused on Jack Manetti, of course, and the S.A.C. told him that recent developments in Kansas City had shown a need to take another look at some previous cases. He asked Hanover if they could interview the staff and have copies of the files for the two cases that had been prosecuted against Jack Manetti, as well as for those dealing with the Stephen Lindsey case.

"Hanover told the S.A.C. that the Lindsey case had been closed with the perpetrator of his murder sentenced to twenty-four years in prison. The S.A.C. kept it vague but indicated they had discovered a connection between Lindsey and some individuals that were being watched in Kansas City. So, they would like to look at any of the files related to the preliminary investigation."

Ellie didn't let on that she already knew about some of this. It was interesting to hear it from both sides.

"Do you know if they were able to get my laptop or the flash drive?" Ellie interrupted.

"Well, yes and no," Cord replied. "Hanover seemed a little surprised when the Lindsey information was mentioned. But he was very cooperative. He called several people into the conference room and introduced each of them, explaining what role they had played in the cases we were interested in. He mentioned that you had been the lead prosecutor but were no longer with the D.A.'s office. He instructed his secretary to see if she could locate your laptop and have it brought to the conference room and instructed the other staff members to cooperate fully with the agents and provide any files or information that was requested as long as it did not compromise any active investigation.

"As part of the interviews, the day you were fired was brought up and we learned that Stephen Lindsey's key chain was given to the Victim's Advocate with instructions to return it to Lindsey's family with any other personal effects that had been held during the investigation into his death. Hanover seemed genuinely surprised when he was told the bullet fob to the key chain was a flash drive. At any rate, the advocate confirmed she had returned the key chain to the family about three days ago.

"Your laptop had been sent down to the IT department to be prepared for another user, which would mean it would be reformatted. Hanover explained that it was policy that the official version of all files be maintained in the central database. So, while he would have his secretary arrange to have the laptop brought to the conference room, any pertinent files should be available in the database and one of the paralegals could help locate them.

"The agents were able to look at the laptop and confirmed it had been completely reformatted. There was nothing like you mentioned in any of the central database files. They have an appointment tomorrow morning with the Lindsey family and will ask about the flash drive at that time."

"Was Hanover interviewed?" Ellie asked.

"Well, I wouldn't call it an interview as much as it was just a wrap up. The S.A.C. always plays his cards close to the vest. He did ask Hanover to elaborate somewhat on your firing. Hanover said only that it was an internal matter and that he could not comment since they had an active investigation in process to ensure the cases you had handled would not leave the D.A.'s office open to allegations of wrongdoing."

Ellie started to interrupt again but Cord held up a hand.

"I know, Ellie, you don't have to say it. But I've got to tell you, without any evidence of the files you saw, it would be your word against Hanover's. The Denver team has forwarded all the files and transcripts from their interviews and the task force will be poring through the information to look for the ties between Lindsey and Carter and any similarities with their deaths. With any luck we'll find information that will allow us to reopen those cases. Apparently, Hanover was so cool and cooperative that the S.A.C. was starting to think it was a wild goose chase and we had been off base with our assessment of what had happened in Lake of the Ozarks and your connection with our investigation."

"But...," Ellie protested.

Once again Cord held up his hand. Ellie's face was turning red; she was about to erupt. She wasn't used to being shushed and she hadn't liked anything she had heard so far. If she was honest with herself, she probably just wanted to yell at Cord since she found out he was engaged. She was beyond frustrated with the whole day.

Cord obviously read Ellie's mood and quickly went on to explain that the Denver S.A.C. had changed his mind as soon as he was back in his office and been briefed on what the team in Kansas City had discovered.

"Look, before I get into this next part, I need to check in with the task force on a couple of things they were working when I left this evening."

Howard stood and told Cord that if he would follow him, he could make the call from his office where he would have some privacy. "Evelyn," he said over his shoulder, "let's move into the great room to hear the rest of what Cord has to tell us."

As soon as the two men were out of the room, Ellie turned to her mother. "Okay, Mother. What are you up to?"

"What am I up to? What would I be up to, Eleanor? I assume you are referring to my conversation with Catherine. She told me that Cord was engaged to a young woman he had known in High School. They had reconnected a couple of years ago when Cord had come back for a visit and they had both attended a charity Christmas event. They've maintained a long-distance relationship since then and became engaged about six months ago. Catherine said she knew the family and everyone was wondering why the couple had not set a date. I was merely trying to help."

"That was a very nice summation, Mother, but save it for a judge and jury. I told you there was nothing between Cord and me and I hope this has convinced you. He's engaged. So, whatever you think is going to happen or that you think you can make happen, you can just forget it right now."

Ellie and her mother had been clearing the table, putting any containers with leftovers into the refrigerator and loading the plates and silverware into the dishwasher. Ellie's mother had also pressed a button on the coffee machine and a carafe of fresh coffee had just finished brewing. She transferred the carafe to a tray, along with some cream and sugar, and motioned to one of the cabinets. Ellie opened the cabinet where she found some coffee mugs. She picked out four mugs and followed her mother into the great room where they placed everything on a low table that was central to one of the seating areas in the room.

It was obvious Evelyn was not going to respond to Ellie's comment. She had taken a seat on the sofa and looked up as Ellie's father came into the great room. "Howard, could you turn on the fire place? There's a little chill in here and I'd rather have the bit of warmth from the fire than fiddle with the thermostat. Besides, we might as well be as comfortable as we can. I have a feeling that this next part is going to be somewhat unpleasant."

CHAPTER 16

Cord entered the room just as Howard had finished setting the gas flame the way he wanted and had taken a seat on the sofa next to Evelyn. All eyes were on Cord as he did a quick survey of the room and walked to one of the chairs placed next to Ellie. He actually repositioned the chair somewhat so that he could look at Ellie as well as her parents. He did not look happy.

"Just say it, Son," Howard encouraged. "Ellie's in danger, isn't she?"

"Yes, Mr. Nelson, I'm afraid so. We're almost certain now that Ellie was the intended target for the shooting down at The Lake. While the activities were taking place in Denver, there were things happening in Kansas City at Tommy Manetti's office. I can't go into all the details but I can tell you that we know Tommy Manetti went kind of crazy this morning. From what we learned, he was in his office reading the morning paper and drinking a cup of coffee. After about fifteen minutes, a crash was heard along with Tommy screaming into the phone. He had apparently thrown the coffee cup against the wall and called a couple of guys that work for him to come to his office immediately. It's not known what was said to the two men but they left shortly after they had been in Manetti's office. Although we haven't been able to prove anything, the two men have been suspects in several assaults. But the victims either refused to press charges or they later claimed they couldn't identify who had attacked them.

"Tommy also made another call, one to his brother. He told Jack there had been a mistake and the package at The Lake wasn't the one he was looking for after all. He told Jack not to worry; he'd find the right package soon. Jack was screaming at Tommy that he couldn't do anything right and asked what kind of people he had working for him. He told Tommy maybe it had been a mistake to put him in charge of the business in Kansas City. Tommy kept assuring him that he'd take care of everything and that he had put his two best men on it."

"So, what are you going to do to protect, Ellie?" Howard asked.

"Wait a minute," Ellie protested. "I don't need protecting. We already talked about this. I can take care of myself and I'm about as safe as I can be with the security we have here."

"For right now, I agree," said Cord. "I don't see any way that the Manetti's could know you are here. They would start looking for you again at The Lake. I've alerted the Sheriff down there of the most recent developments and advised him to keep an eye out for any suspicious activity around your house. They have only a handful of deputies covering a large area, but he did say he would increase the patrol in your neighborhood. Once again, I think that gives us a day or two and I'm hoping we'll find something soon in the files we got from Denver or from the interviews we'll be doing tomorrow."

"Who are you talking to tomorrow?" Ellie asked.

"As I mentioned earlier, the team in Denver will be going to the Lindsey house to see if they can recover the flash drive. Depending on the results from that and the analysis of the D.A. Investigator's files, a visit to Lindsey's office or to the Denver Police Department may also happen. Here, in Kansas City, we've got Rob Carter's partner coming in for an interview and we're going to be talking to the Kansas City Police to provide us with the files on Carter's death to determine if we can make a tie into our investigation and determine if the case should be reopened.

"We should know a lot more tomorrow. In the meantime, Ellie should stay put. I'll plan to give you an update again tomorrow evening and we can go from there."

Cord stood and directed his last comments to Ellie's father. "Rest assured, Mr. Nelson, if it is determined that Ellie is in immediate danger, I will personally see to it that she has someone assigned to protect her, whether she wants it or not."

Howard got up, walked over and shook Cord's hand. "I'll hold you to that, Son. Come on this way, I'll grab your coat and show you out. We'll just plan for you to come back over the same time tomorrow for dinner."

Ellie just sat there with her mouth hanging open. It appeared no one was paying attention to her and what she wanted. Even her mother wasn't saying anything and, instead, was busying herself clearing away the coffee that no one had touched.

So, that's how it was going to be. She was perfectly capable of taking care of herself and she was going to start acting like it.

"It's been a long day, Mother, I think I'll go on up to my room."

When Ellie got to her room, she shut the door and went over to her desk. She opened the MacBook and brought up the browser. It was true that she was tired. But her anger had given her a burst of energy and she had some research she wanted to do. She had no intention of sitting around the house the next day like someone afraid of their own shadow. The F.B.I. was very good at what they did but they were typically slow moving. Information was analyzed and sent up the chain of command, where decisions were made, and approved actions came back down the chain to the field agents. The task force probably simplified things somewhat, but Ellie wanted the threat over her to end sooner rather than later. She had a couple of ideas how she could help move things along.

She quickly subscribed to the Kansas City Star and began searching for articles related to Gino Russo and Rob Carter's death.

Gino Russo had died of natural causes. There had been a couple of articles around the time of his death. The first recounted that he had been the CEO of Midwest Enterprises and that he had been in poor health. It stated he had a weak heart and had suffered a mild heart attack about six months prior to the massive one that caused his death. The second article had a little different flavor. It went into a little more detail about his businesses and suspected ties to organized crime. Midwest Enterprises consisted of several businesses, with the two primary operations being a waste management company and a laundry and dry-cleaning service. Tommy Manetti had been named as the new CEO of Midwest Enterprises.

Rob Carter's death was a different matter. The first headline screamed: PROMINENT KANSAS CITY ATTORNEY FALLS TO HIS DEATH. The article gave the initial information that he had fallen from the rooftop of the garage adjacent to the law firm where he was a partner. As with any accident, the death was under investigation. There were follow-up articles for a few days that eerily paralleled those for the Lindsey death in Denver. Both attorneys, both fell or were pushed from a garage rooftop. Rob Carter's death was originally thought suspicious, but was eventually ruled a suicide. Carter's law partner had said that the man had been depressed since the death of Gino Russo, who was his primary client. Not only was Carter losing Russo's personal business but also that of Midwest Enterprises. The new CEO was keeping his account with the firm but had requested that it be handled by the firm's other partner. Carter's wife had been adamant that he would not have committed suicide and that they were planning a long overdue vacation to the Bahamas.

Ellie finished reading the articles and did a search of the law firm. She read about the firm and the information about its partners and associates. She picked up her phone and entered the address into the GPS app. Cord had mentioned that the partner was being interviewed at F.B.I. headquarters the next day. Ellie planned to take advantage of the partner's absence and see if she could get some information out of the support staff, starting with Carter's secretary. Like most offices, the secretaries generally knew a lot more about what was going on than they were given credit for, particularly by the old boys' club that was alive and well within the legal profession, as well as within the F.B.I. Ellie knew all about the glass ceiling and she had taken the time at each level of her career to understand the contribution made by each member of the D.A.'s staff, male or female. She had no doubt that she could connect with Carter's secretary...if she could get in to see her or him.

Satisfied that she had a good plan for the next day, Ellie closed the MacBook and got ready for bed. She slipped under the comforter and her head had no sooner hit the pillow than she was out like a light.

CHAPTER 17

L ight filtering into the room awakened Ellie and she looked at the clock on the table beside the bed. 9:00 a.m. Goodness, she had slept longer than she had intended. She was going to have to get a move on if she was going to get to Carter's firm before lunch. First, she needed coffee.

Ellie went in her pajamas and bare feet down the stairs and into the kitchen. The coffee machine was already set up. She silently thanked her mother or father, whichever one had thoughtfully had the machine ready, and pushed the button to start the brew. While waiting for the coffee to finish, she noticed a note on the table. Her mother had written that both she and Ellie's father planned to be at their offices all day. As with the day before, dinner was planned for 6:30, but this time her father was going to pick up the take-out. Ellie smiled at the postscript under her mother's signature. It had been written by her father and read, "You'll love 'em...best burritos ever!"

After grabbing a mug of coffee, Ellie went back to her room and stood inside the walk-in closet, sipping her coffee and surveying her clothes for what would be the right thing to wear. She finally decided on a pair of wool slacks, a turtleneck and a tweed jacket. That should keep her looking business-like but project the friendly vibe she was going for. While there was still some snow on the sides of the road, the streets and sidewalks were dry and the temperature was actually expected to get up into the sixties. She was hoping the tweed jacket would be all the coat she would need.

She took a quick shower, put on her makeup, did a quick blow dry of her hair and got dressed. As she checked herself out in the full-length mirror in the back of her closet, she was pleased with the look and was even happier to notice she no longer had the dark circles under her eyes. It was amazing what a good night's sleep, a little concealer and a renewed sense of purpose could do. It was true; if you looked good, you'd feel good and the reverse was also true. She grabbed her phone and the keys to the Cayenne and headed downstairs.

When Ellie went into the kitchen, she rinsed out her coffee mug and put it in the dishwasher. She searched through the cabinets and found a travel mug that she filled with coffee before shutting off the machine and walking through the mudroom into the garage. As she drove down the driveway and waited for the gate to open, she pulled up the GPS app on her phone. She followed the directions until the automated voice from the app said, "Your destination is on the left."

She drove passed the front of the building and then turned into the adjacent parking garage. She thought about going all the way to the roof but decided that wasn't going to help her since she really didn't have any details regarding which side of the roof Carter had jumped from. Instead she found a spot on the second level that had a connecting walkway into the office building where Carter's law firm was located. She double checked the building directory and then took one of the elevators to the sixteenth floor. When the elevator stopped, Ellie exited and saw a set of glass double doors to her right. Through the glass could be seen a reception area with a young woman sitting behind a rather massive desk. Ellie already had her story ready and a name picked out for the receptionist who was watching Ellie approach. The receptionist greeted her as soon as she walked through the doors.

"May I help you?"

"Yes, my name is Olivia Bennett. I don't have an appointment but I was wondering if I might be able to see Mr. Carter."

"I'm sorry. That won't be possible."

"Oh, I know it's a bit presumptuous, but he and my father went to law school together. If you tell him Dan Bennett's daughter would like to see him..."

"No, you don't understand. I am sorry to be the one to tell you but Mr. Carter has passed away."

Ellie pretended to be shocked. "Oh my, I had no idea and am sure my father did not know that either. He'll be very upset that he had not been in touch recently. What happened? Is there someone I can talk to...his partner or his secretary? I'd like to be able to give my father some details."

The receptionist told her to have a seat and she would see if someone was free to talk with her. A few minutes later, a young woman entered the reception. The term "blond bombshell" came to mind. Although she was dressed conservatively, the business suit couldn't hide what was obviously a very voluptuous figure. Her hair and makeup were expertly done. But she didn't quite come off as sophisticated. She had too much youthful exuberance and you could almost sense a touch of naivete as she walked over to where Ellie was sitting. Ellie started to stand but the woman motioned her to stay seated and took a seat next to her.

"I'm Ashley. I believe Jessica said your name is Olivia. Is that right?"

"Yes, Olivia Bennett. I just can't believe Mr. Carter is dead. My father always spoke very highly of him. Did you work with him?"

"I was his secretary. It has been very difficult, especially since it was a suicide. You always wonder if you should have noticed something that would have made a difference."

"Suicide? Oh, my father is really going to be devastated. This is just so hard to comprehend. I wonder if I could treat you to lunch and we could talk a bit more? It would really help me be able to make sense of this for my father."

Ellie hoped she wasn't laying it on too thick and that they had bought her story. Ashley seemed to hesitate for a minute but then told Ellie she couldn't take too long since things were still in a bit of chaos. She suggested they walk to a deli that was just about a half block away. Ellie stood and waited in the reception area until Ashley returned with her coat and told the receptionist she would be back in under an hour.

As they made their way to the deli, Ellie asked Ashley how long she had worked for Rob Carter.

"Oh, I was hired a little over two years ago. My boyfriend got me the job and it was wonderful working for Mr. Carter. He was always so nice. It was just a total shock. First, Mr. Russo and then Mr. Carter."

"Mr. Russo, is that someone else at your firm?" Ellie asked, pretending she didn't know the name.

"Oh, Mr. Russo was Mr. Carter's client and he was also my boyfriend's boss. Mr. Russo died and Mr. Carter committed suicide right after that because he was so upset."

They reached the deli and placed their orders at the counter. Ellie had decided she might have lucked out with Ashley. Ashley definitely liked to talk.

They sat at one of the tables and Ellie continued to ask questions.

"Did Mr. Russo commit suicide too?"

"Oh, no, Mr. Russo had a heart attack. He and Mr. Carter had worked together for years, but when he died, there were changes made at Mr. Russo's company. I mean it was good for my Joey, that's my boyfriend. When the new CEO took over, my Joey was promoted. But the CEO decided he wanted Mr. Martin to handle their accounts instead of Mr. Carter. So, that's the other reason they are saying Mr. Carter committed suicide."

The food was delivered to the table and then nothing was said for a few minutes while they began eating their food. Eventually, Ashley broke the silence.

"You never told me where you were from, Olivia."

"I'm from Denver," Ellie replied.

"Wow," said Ashley, "That's interesting. You're the second person from Denver that I've had to talk to about Mr. Carter's death."

"It's a small world. Maybe I know the person. Do you remember the person's name?

"Yes, it was a man named Lindsey. I only remember because I had mailed a package to him from Mr. Carter a few days before and here he was calling and I had to tell him Mr. Carter was dead. It was very upsetting. When I told my Joey about it that night, he took me out to dinner to help me take my mind off everything. I don't know how I would have gotten through all this without my Joey."

Ashley signaled a nearby waiter and asked for a to go box. Ellie took the hint. She was starting to get the picture and she thought she had better not press her luck any further.

"I should probably get going and let you get back to work. I am really sorry for your loss, Ashley. Thank you so much for talking with me. It will be much easier for me to tell my father now."

With that Ellie picked up the check and went to the cashier to pay. She and Ashley left the deli together, said their good-byes, and went their separate ways. Ashley headed back to her office building. Ellie purposely turned the other direction and went into a nearby store. After she was sure Ashley had enough time to go into her building, she walked back to the parking garage.

CHAPTER 18

When Ellie got back to the house, she grabbed a bottled water from the refrigerator and went up to her room. She changed into a pair of leggings and a t-shirt and sat down at her desk. She had new information she wanted to add to the notes she had made before and she wanted to transfer the information from the legal pad into digital form on her MacBook.

She opened up the PowerPoint app and began adding the text, boxes and connecting arrows needed to copy what she had on her sheet of paper. Satisfied with the way it looked. She then began adding the new information.

Originally, she had just shown a connection between Carter's and Lindsey's names with their law school connection. Now she had some of the pieces missing from her original chart. It was likely that Carter had sent Lindsey papers with his shorthand notes and that Lindsey had scanned the papers at some point and saved them to the flash drive. Ellie suspected that the original set of papers was long gone but that they were what got Lindsey killed.

After her talk with Ashley, she also had a pretty good idea how the Manetti's made the connection between Carter and Lindsey. It had been Ashley telling her boyfriend the same thing she had told Ellie. The boyfriend had obviously passed the information on to Tommy Manetti who, in turn, passed it on to his brother Jack. Jack would have been the one to arrange the hit on Lindsey and have Harpo either commit the murder himself or convince him to take the fall.

Ellie added in the remaining names and arrows to capture all that and she felt she had a pretty clear picture how everything had happened. She planned to tell Cord that night about the new information. She couldn't wait to find out if the F.B.I. had been able to talk to Lindsey's family and recover the flash drive.

A glance at the system clock displayed in the corner of the MacBook told Ellie she'd been working on her notes for longer than she thought. She still had a couple of hours before everyone would show up for dinner but decided she might as well go downstairs and get things ready. And she could sure use a cup of coffee.

Ellie did a quick check in the mirror and decided she was good to go. She'd have time to run back upstairs before Cord got there and put on some lip gloss, but other than that she was determined not to go out of her way to try and impress him. After all, he was taken. Ellie was surprised at how disappointed she was at that thought. Well, she'd just have to get over it.

She grabbed her phone, opened her messaging app, and sent a text asking her friend Lisa if she was free to chat. She wanted to fill Lisa in on what was happening and see if there was anything new at the D.A.s office. She also had been thinking a lot about what she wanted to do with her life and she was certain she did not want to return to Denver. That meant she was going to need to do something about her condo, her furniture, and her car, not to mention her clothes. She had quite a few things at her parents' house, but not nearly everything she would like to have. Plus, she really missed painting and wanted her easel and paints. The last items meant she was also going to have to get a place of her own sooner rather than later. An idea was beginning to form on where it was going to be, but she wasn't quite ready to share that part yet.

Ellie had reached the kitchen and had just started setting the table when her cell phone rang. The display showed it was Lisa.

"Hey, Lisa. How are you doing? And how are things at work today?"

"I'm doing okay and things are much quieter at work today. Hanover has been in his office all day with the door shut. The F.B.I. agents haven't shown today but they said they might be scheduling some follow up interviews after they have had time to look through all the files we copied for them. On a personal note, I've got a date with Sam tonight. He's that Systems Engineer that works with the IT guys. I hope there's some good stuff to tell about that tomorrow. So, what's going on with you? Anything new with you and the hunky F.B.I. guy?"

Ellie continued to set the table with one hand as she held her cell in the other. She filled Lisa in about what she had learned at Carter's law firm and that she hoped she would hear from Cord later that night that the F.B.I. in Denver had recovered Lindsey's flash drive.

"Ooh, you're going to see Cord again? That's what I want to know more about."

"Nothing to know. It turns out he's engaged. He has a fiancée in Boston."

"Well, engaged isn't married and Boston is a long way from Kansas City. You're there and she is not. Sounds to me like there's plenty of opportunity there. I say go for it!"

"You know me. You know I would never do that. I'd be lying though if I didn't say I wished the circumstances were different. But I'm only saying that to you and I'll deny we ever had this conversation if you tell anyone else."

The last comment got the chuckle from Lisa she was going for and it allowed her to change the subject.

"Lisa, I've decided I'm going to move back here to Missouri when this is all over. I have a proposition for you. I know you're saving up to buy a condo.

Would you be interested in renting my condo from me? In exchange for you helping me pack up my stuff and ship a few things now and then, I'd just ask you to pay the utilities and HOA fees and I'll continue to pay the mortgage. That way you can save up some money and after a year, you can decide if you want to buy the condo from me or find a different place. How does that sound?"

"Well, I don't like the fact that you are moving because I'll miss you. But I'd be crazy not to take your offer. Are you sure? And what are you going to do about your car?"

"Yes, I'm sure. It actually works for me because I don't know if I want to buy something here right now. I've got a couple of ideas rolling around in my head. It would really help to hear myself talk out loud to someone about them. So, that brings me to what to do about my car. I thought I would fly into Denver, pack the car with some clothes, my paints, and easel and drive it back here. I was hoping you could take some vacation and ride back with me. The bad part is you'd have to listen to me; the good part is you'll get some downtime. I know it's been crazy for you at work lately."

"That sounds great, Ellie. When do you want to do this?"

"I think that depends on what happens in the next few days. Maybe I'll know more tomorrow. I'll call you then. Don't forget I want the scoop on your hot date."

Just as Ellie was hanging up the phone. The intercom buzzed signaling someone was at the front gate. Ellie pushed the speaker button. "Can I help you?"

"Ellie, this is Cord."

Ellie pushed the button that would open the gate and then walked toward the front of the house. She checked herself in the hallway mirror and did a quick finger comb to fluff out her hair. She wasn't going to have time to put on any lip gloss. Well, what did it matter now anyway.

"He's engaged. He's engaged. He's engaged." Ellie repeated to herself as she opened the front door.

CHAPTER 19

The door was barely opened when Cord stormed through.

"What did you do? Are you crazy?"

Ellie could clearly see Cord was agitated. Somehow, he must have found out about her visit to Carter's law firm. She didn't want to get into it right there in the foyer. So, she put on a sweet smile and said, "Well, good afternoon to you also, Special Agent Sinclair. Won't you give me your coat? You are a bit early, but we can go on into the kitchen and chat."

"Chat? Chat? You bet we'll chat. You were supposed to stay here out of sight. What were you thinking?"

Ignoring him again, Ellie held out her hands for his coat. Cord stared hard at Ellie for a moment, took off his coat, and as he handed it to her, he spoke with more than a touch of sarcasm.

"Why, thank you, Miss Nelson. I'd love to join you in the kitchen. Perhaps we could have some tea and you can tell me about your day."

Neither of them spoke as Ellie hung up Cord's coat in the hall closet. She turned and walked toward the kitchen. She could feel Cord practically on her heels and she could still fill the anger coming off him. As far as Ellie was concerned, there was no reason for him to be so bent out of shape. She wasn't used to someone questioning her actions and if Cord thought he was going to intimidate her, he'd better think again.

It was like a standoff in a western movie. They walked through the kitchen and each took up a position on either side of the breakfast nook table. Both stood still, gripping the back of the chair and glaring at each other.

After what seemed like an eternity, Cord's expression softened. He seemed to have come to a decision. He pulled out the chair and sat.

"Okay, let's start again. I apologize for barging in here like I did, but I'm worried about you."

"I can handle..." Ellie started.

"Normally, I'm sure you can handle yourself," Cord interrupted. "But I don't think you understand these people are playing for keeps. A body was fished out of the Kaw River. It was a thug named Ralph Riva. He had a rap sheet a mile long. Our sources tell us that he worked for the Manetti's and did whatever they asked him to do; emphasis on the whatever. We know that he was at Manetti's office the day after Doug Withers was shot down at The Lake. It is too coincidental that he turned up dead the next day. Although we don't have proof yet, our guess is that he was the shooter and that he paid a big price for hitting the wrong target.

"They got the wrong target. You are the target. That's why you were supposed to stay out of sight and we should have had a couple of days before they clued into the fact that you weren't still at The Lake. I don't know what you did. But they know you are in Kansas City. And it's probably just a matter of time before they figure out where you are. I'm worried that will put not only you but also your parents in jeopardy."

"Oh," said Ellie somewhat meekly, "You really think they would go after my parents? I don't even know why they are so intent in killing me. I don't have anything that would incriminate them. What little I saw in Carter's files would only be hearsay and supposition in court."

"I think they are tying up loose ends no matter what or where they are. Our agents went to Lindsey's home yesterday to ask about the flash drive. It turns out that Mrs. Lindsey had no idea the bullet on the key chain was a flash drive. When the Victim's Advocate returned the key chain, Mrs. Lindsey just put it in a desk drawer."

"Oh, good, you got it then!" Ellie cried.

"No, that's just it. We didn't get it. There had been a burglary the day after the key chain had been returned. All the TVs and computer equipment in the house were stolen. They didn't take anything else in the house, not even the jewelry. So, Mrs. Lindsey was surprised when she went to the office to get the key chain for the agents. It wasn't there. Since she was sure that was where she put it and she hadn't moved it, she said it must have been stolen during the burglary and she just hadn't noticed it. When the agents left, Mrs. Lindsey wasn't the only one wondering why all this was happening.

"The agents checked with the Denver Police and they verified the information about the burglary and what had been taken. The police had been watching pawn shops to see if any of the items had turned up, but so far, nothing.

"So, we're back to square one with finding Carter's files and you are still very much a loose end. They obviously don't want to take even the slightest chance you know something that may cause them a problem. Now, tell me how Manetti knows you are in KC."

"Okay. But I've got to have some coffee. Would you like some? I can make an espresso, a latte, or an Americano. It'll only take a minute but the machine makes a bit of noise. I promise I'll tell you what I've learned right after that."

Cord said he'd have whatever she was having. Ellie went to the Verismo machine, filled the water reservoir, and reached into the cabinet for the container with the single-serving espresso pods. She selected a Columbian medium roast espresso and inserted the pod into the machine. After setting a mug under the spout, she pressed the button to extract the espresso from the pod and then pressed the button that would send a measured amount of water into the cup to make it an Americano. She repeated the process for the second cup and then carried both mugs over to the table, setting one in front of Cord.

Finally, Ellie sat, took a calming sip of her coffee, and then told Cord how she had used a fake name and had talked with Carter's secretary, pretending that she hadn't known that Carter was dead. She told him her theory about the series of events that led to Lindsey's murder and that Ashley was more than likely just a pawn in the whole thing. Ellie's take was that she was a sweet girl and would be genuinely upset if she knew how she was being used.

"Well, that explains how Manetti would have known you were here," said Cord when Ellie had finished. "A fake name wasn't nearly enough to disguise who you are. That red hair is a dead giveaway. Hopefully, that won't become a literal expression.

"From your description of Ashley, my guess is she couldn't wait to get on the phone with Joey and tell him all about her interesting visitor. It was probably Joey who made a phone call to Manetti saying they thought the package he had been looking for wasn't at The Lake at all and was here in Kansas City. The person said the package had the wrong address but he was pretty sure it was the right one and he'd have someone check it out and get back to Manetti.

"The wrong address obviously referred to the phony name you used but he must have asked Ashley to describe you. I don't like this at all. We didn't get the flash drive and we didn't get any new information from Carter's law partner, Victor Martin. He claimed no knowledge of any tie between Rob Carter and Stephen Lindsey. I'm going to pass along the information you learned from Carter's secretary and we will most definitely call her in for an interview. But I'm afraid without any evidence of the files Carter sent to Lindsey, this isn't going to get us anywhere closer to making a case against either Manetti. And you're in just as much danger, if not more."

Cord seemed to be thinking out loud as much as talking to her. He was clearly agitated again as he mentioned the danger to her. He stood up from his chair, frowning at Ellie. She got the feeling he expected her to say something and when she didn't, he let out an exasperated sigh.

"Can I use your father's den again? If you'll excuse me for a few minutes, I've got to call my team, bring them up to date, and see what we want to do with the information you got from Carter's secretary."

"Sure, go ahead and use dad's den. Both he and my mother should be home in a few minutes. I'll let dad know you're in there. He said he was picking up some burritos. So, come on out when you're finished and you can join us for dinner."

CHAPTER 20

When Cord returned to the kitchen, Ellie and her parents were just sitting down at the table.

"Just in time, Cord," Howard Nelson said. "You are in for a treat. I picked up burritos at Manny's. Are you done for the day? I can get you a beer to go with it, if you'd like."

"I wasn't going to impose another night, but you've twisted my arm. I can't turn down something from Manny's. And, yes, I'd like a beer. You all stay seated and I'll grab it from the fridge if that's okay."

"That'll be good. Ellie has filled us in on everything that has gone on today. I understand you think we might be in danger here. But I think it's safe to say nothing is going to happen right at this moment. So, let's enjoy our dinner and we can talk over coffee afterward if there is a need."

Ellie smirked a little as she watched her father steamrolling over any conversation Cord might have wanted to start. She was certain Cord could pull out a tough F.B.I. persona if he so chose. But her father was also used to being in control and he was a pretty formidable man in his own right. Cord was smart enough to know when to press an issue and when not to.

They all dove into the beef burritos and talked about safe subjects like the upcoming Chiefs and Broncos game and the Plaza Christmas light display that would be turned on the following week on Thanksgiving night.

They had just finished dinner when Ellie's phone buzzed in her pocket. She pulled it out and saw a text from her friend, Lisa. It said: Call me 911!!!!

"Something's wrong. It's Lisa. I need to call her now," said Ellie as she speed-dialed Lisa's number.

"Ellie, Ellie!" Lisa cried as soon as the call went through. "Is Cord there? You have to tell him!"

"Slow down, Lisa. Are you okay?"

"Yes, yes, I'm okay. It's just that I think we may have a copy of those files you saved on your laptop. Is Cord there? You need to tell him."

"What are you talking about? I thought you were out on a date tonight?

"I was. I mean, I am. Sam's great. We were having dinner, and naturally, we started talking about the day the F.B.I. showed up here. So, Sam is a Systems Engineer in the IT department. So, I mentioned that I had seen Matt bring up your old laptop and give it to the F.B.I. but it had already been formatted and there was nothing on it. And Sam said sure that was the procedure, but the procedure also calls for them to physically remove the hard drive and put in a new one. The old hard drive is kept in the archives so the files can be retrieved if a case is questioned at some future time. They didn't tell Matt what they wanted the laptop for and the IT department is so busy with year-end maintenance stuff that Sam figured it wouldn't have even crossed Matt's mind to mention the hard drive.

"Sam and I are super excited. He says the whole department is working overtime and everyone but him is still over at the building working late. He had called in a favor to get the time off to have dinner with me. But we're on our way over there now. Sam says he can look for the hard drive, no problem. Can Cord send someone over to get it? It'll take us about forty-five minutes to get downtown to the building."

Listening to Lisa, Ellie was excited, too. She told Lisa to hold on and quickly related the information to Cord.

Cord wasted no time making a call of his own to one of the task force members in Denver. He quickly passed along the information and the agent he was talking to agreed to meet Lisa and Sam. He passed his phone to Ellie and had her give the agent Lisa's cell phone number. As Ellie was speaking to the Denver agent, Cord motioned for Ellie to hand him her phone.

"Lisa, this is Cord. Ellie is giving your cell phone information to Agent Jackson. He'll be calling you in just a minute to arrange to meet you and go into the building together. If the hard drive is there, we'll need to maintain the chain of evidence. So, wait for Agent Jackson. And, Lisa, thanks to you and Sam. I'm giving you back to Ellie."

Ellie and Cord switched phones and Ellie quickly ended her call with Lisa.

"Good luck. Call me!"

Cord asked Agent Jackson to give him a call back once it was determined if they had the drive and he'd have a plan in place to have someone access and transcribe the files for analysis.

"Maybe we're finally catching a break," said Cord after he had ended the call. "Look it's going to be a while before they get to the building and locate the hard drive. I've got to go so I can set up a call with the Denver and Kansas City task force members and get things ready to set in motion."

"Cord, if they find it, the files are in a folder called Silver Bullet."

"Thanks, Ellie, I'll let Jackson know."

You could feel the excitement in the room. Everyone knew if the F.B.I. had Carter's files, it would no longer just be Ellie's word the files existed and that should be enough to get the target off her back.

Cord thanked the Nelson's for dinner and hurried toward the front door, telling them he'd grab his own coat. Seconds later he was gone.

"I'm going to put on a pot of coffee," said Evelyn. "I, for one, am not planning to go anywhere until we hear back from Lisa."

Ellie busied herself clearing the remains of the dinner from the table. When the coffee was ready, they each poured themselves a mug and sat back down at the table. Ellie listened in silence as her parents chatted back and forth about their day. They all sipped their coffee as they talked and although no one said anything, each of them occasionally glanced over at Ellie's phone sitting on the table. It was as if they were trying to will it to ring.

When it finally did ring, it startled them. Howard and Evelyn watched anxiously as Ellie grabbed the phone.

"Lisa, how did it go? Was it there? Tell me what happened."

"Yes. It was there. Agent Jackson met us in the parking garage and we all went up to the IT department. Sam worked with Matt to bring up the online record that showed which hard drive came from your laptop and where it was stored. Once they physically got the hard drive, Matt had to decrypt it and did a quick check to verify it contained files that could be attributed to you. Agent Jackson was recording and photographing everything that was happening. Once they verified it was yours, Agent Jackson asked them to look for a Silver Bullet folder.

It was there, Ellie; it looked just like what you described.

"We didn't get to look at it for long though. Agent Jackson took it as soon as he could see there was information in the folder. I'm watching him leave now and he's got his phone to his ear. I'm guessing he is calling Cord.

"I've got to say, I like Sam and we were having a great time. I think we're going to set another date, but it's going to be hard to top this one. This was all pretty exciting and the best thing is you'll be safe now. Right?"

"That's what I'm hoping. I guess we'll know more once the F.B.I. transcribes the files and word gets out that they have them. Thank you *so* much, Lisa. I've got to go now and fill in my mom and dad. I'll talk to you tomorrow."

Ellie hung up and told her parents everything Lisa had said.

"Thank God!" Evelyn said as she stood up from the table. This has been quite a day. I think I'm going to head on upstairs and call it a night. How about you, Howard?"

"That sounds like a good idea. Maybe I'll flip on the History Channel and see where they are in finding that treasure up in Canada."

Each of her parents gave Ellie a quick hug as they passed her on the way to the staircase. "Try to put it aside, Eleanor," her mother added as she gave her a quick peck on the cheek. "You need to get some rest, too. This has been more of a strain for you than you probably realize."

It took Ellie only a minute to decide her mother was right. She headed up to her room.

CHAPTER 21

Ellie changed out of her clothes, put on a sleep shirt and propped herself up in bed with her MacBook on her lap. The F.B.I. now had her hard drive and she had no doubt that they would have a team of people looking at it. The problem was how long that might take. First, they would have to transcribe the shorthand in Carter's files. Then, they would have to compare it against the other data the task force had. That would lead to more analysis on how they should proceed. Finally, any recommendation would be sent up the chain of command for approval to act.

Meanwhile, Ellie was still a target and her life was on hold. She wasn't going to sit back and wait for the

F.B.I. to put a case together. She thought back to the two cases she had prosecuted against Jack Manetti in Denver. Now that she knew there was a strong tie between Denver and Kansas City, she wondered if that was the reason the trail always seemed to go cold. The witness for the Jack Manetti murder charge was still officially listed as missing. Everyone thought at the time the witness was most likely dead. But a body had never surfaced. Maybe a body was never found because they were looking in Denver when they should have been looking in Kansas City.

Ellie was frustrated that she didn't have access to her files in Denver and that she'd only had a brief glimpse of the files that Rob Carter had sent to Stephen Lindsey. But she had seen enough to know that there were dates that coincided with times she had prosecuted Jack Manetti. She knew it was only speculation, but what if Rob Carter was uneasy with Tommy Manetti as Russo's second in command. What if he kept a file on Tommy and that file also had information about the connections to Denver. What if Tommy had found out about the file, probably through Ashley's boyfriend. Then, when Russo died, Tommy had Carter killed.

That was a lot of "what ifs" but Ellie thought she was on the right track. She opened her MacBook and brought up her subscription to the Kansas City Star. She entered in a two-week search parameter beginning the day after her witness in Denver had gone missing. She tried several different keyword combinations and, finally, found what she wanted when she entered John Doe.

The headline read JOHN DOE PULLED FROM KAW. Ellie was excited because she remembered that Cord had said they'd recently pulled a body from the Kaw. That body was the man they suspected had been the shooter sent by Manetti to kill her. There was more than a year between the two discoveries, but Ellie was convinced if one was tied to the Manetti's, so was the other one.

There wasn't much to the article, but it was enough as far as Ellie was concerned. An unidentified body had been found by a man fishing along the banks of the river. The body had been in the river for at least three days and the police had been unsuccessful in making an identification. The article had ended with a request for anyone with information to contact the Kansas City, Kansas, police department.

Ellie found that last part interesting and she could see where it might have added another layer of confusion. People not from Kansas City almost always thought it was in Kansas. And it is true there is a Kansas City, Kansas. But the major metropolis is on the Missouri side. The two cities are separated where the Kansas (referred to locally as the Kaw) and Missouri rivers join and they could not be more different. The residents in both cities are sensitive to the issue and it's just another bone of contention that has been wedged between the two states since before the civil war.

Now that Ellie suspected the unidentified body might be the missing witness from her case against Jack Manetti, she had to decide what to do about it. But there was nothing she could do about it then. It would have to wait until morning. She closed the MacBook and set it on the nightstand beside her bed. She leaned her head back on the pillow and almost immediately fell asleep. Unfortunately, it was a fitful sleep.

Ellie roused herself from bed the minute she saw the early dawn light seeping into her room. What she needed was a run. The solitude of a run in the early morning was the perfect time for her to think through what her brain had refused to let go of during the night. Typical of Missouri in November, there was no sign of the freaky snow storm of the previous week and Kansas City was currently enjoying spring-like weather. A quick check of the weather app on her cell phone told Ellie it was already fifty degrees out and would get up to the mid-sixties. She quickly put on a pair of leggings and a t-shirt and added a hoodie. She put her cell phone in her hoodie pocket and laced up her tennis shoes. She quietly made her way downstairs, grabbed a set of keys from the rack in the mud room and exited though the garage.

After some brief stretching, Ellie unlocked the gate that was next to the driveway entrance and stepped out onto the sidewalk. As soon as she heard the gate click shut, she started out at a fast jog toward Loose Park. The park was only about a block away and had a path that circled the entire park. Ellie hoped there wouldn't be many other joggers out at this time of the morning and she'd have the solitude she loved.

The sound of an engine starting up somewhere behind her made the hairs on the back of Ellie's neck stand up. She looked back to see a dark SUV pulling out from the curb. She had a very bad feeling. Even though she was only about a half block from the park she knew the car would catch up with her before she could make it there. She couldn't go back the way she'd come so she decided to use her knowledge of the neighborhood to her advantage.

Ellie darted to her left, running away from the street and across the lawn of the nearest house. The Parker's lived there and they had a pool house in the back. She ran across a stone patio, skirted the pool and made her way to the back side of the pool house. She stopped and stood with her back to the wall, trying to catch her breath. While straining for any sounds that someone had followed her through the yard, she pulled out her cell phone and punched the contact button to dial Cord.

"Ellie?" Cord answered.

"Cord," Ellie whispered, "I need help."

"What's the matter? Where are you? I was just about to pull up into your driveway."

"Black SUV following me. Brick colonial. Two houses down. I'm in the back."

"Stay on the line. I'll be right there."

Cord's eyes scanned the road in front of him and he saw a black SUV idling about half a block away.

The driver of the SUV must have been watching in his rear-view mirror because as soon as Cord punched the gas, there was a loud squeal and the SUV burned rubber, leaving a trail of smoke behind as it sped to the end of the block, made a right turn and quickly was gone from sight.

Ellie was his main concern so he didn't even think about chasing after the car. He turned into the driveway of the house Ellie had described.

"Okay, Ellie, I'm in front of the garage and the SUV is gone. Where are you? You can come out."

Cord got out of his car and began scanning the area behind the house, he saw Ellie step out from behind a pool house and start running toward him. Cord took quick strides across the patio, closing the distance between them. As Ellie reached him, he didn't even hesitate. He folded her into his arms and held her until she stopped trembling.

"I'm sorry," Ellie said softly as she stepped back out of Cord's embrace. She fully expected Cord to be angry with her, but as she looked up to meet his eyes, she saw only relief. She had an urge to step back into the warmth of his body and kiss him to let him know she was all right. Once again, she had to remind herself he was engaged and there was no way she would show her feelings. Instead, she took another step backwards to put more distance between them and to break the moment.

"I suppose I deserve a lecture. What were you doing here so early? Not that I'm complaining, I'm really glad you were here and scared those guys off."

Ellie's tone was stronger and it achieved her goal of breaking the moment between her and Cord. Based on Cord's next words, maybe she had done too good a job. A deep frown now appeared on Cord's face.

"Damned right you deserve a lecture. What were you thinking?"

"That's just it. I needed to think. Jogging helps me think. After I knew you had the hard drive from my laptop, I thought I'd no longer be a target. Of course, I realize now that just because I know you have the hard drive, it doesn't mean the bad guys know you have it. Obviously, they are still looking for me. I'm glad you were here. Why were you here?"

Cord sighed and pointed to his car. "Get in. I'll drive you back to your house."

They got into the car and Cord backed down the Parker's driveway and out into the street. Other than the code needed to open the gate, neither had spoken until they had driven through the gate and were parked in front of the garage doors.

"I was here because I called in a couple of favors and I asked an agent to monitor your parents' house. But he couldn't be here until eight this morning. I was up early. So, I decided to be on the safe side, I would come here myself until he showed up to take over. I'm glad I did.

"I was going to come talk to you anyway. If you are willing, we'd like to bring you in as a consultant on the task force to help analyze the information on your hard drive. Since the hard drive had been in your possession, we want you to confirm the contents for traceability and to give any insights you have that could help us make a case against the Manetti's."

Ellie didn't hesitate in accepting the offer. "That's perfect. I found some information last night and it was difficult putting events and information together by memory. If I can look at the files on my hard drive, I think I just might have something that would help. How are we going to do this?"

"You're going to need to come with me to the F.B.I. office and I can set you up a space where the task force is working. I'm guessing you are going to want to change. How soon can you be ready?"

"I'm going to need a half hour. Do you want to come in for coffee?"

"No thanks. I've got some calls to make to ensure everyone that needs to be is brought up to date on what happened here this morning, not the least of which is the agent that should be showing up in a few minutes. I also need to let the task force know you'll be joining us and have your clearance and a laptop set up. I'll be out here when you're ready and we'll just need to make a quick stop by my place."

As Ellie got out of the car, Cord added, "Be sure to tell your folks that there will be an agent monitoring the house and it might be a good idea if they carpool together for a couple of days. If they sense any problems, they can call my number and we can get someone to them within minutes."

CHAPTER 22

It took Ellie more like 45 minutes, but she had wanted to make sure she looked like the confident, capable person she was. She felt better than she had in days. She was used to being in control and moving from point A to B to C to a logical conclusion. Being able to look at her files would go a long way toward getting some order back in her life.

She had found a tailored dark blue pinstripe suit in the closet that she paired with a white button-down collared oxford shirt. Although the suit was a couple of years old, it was a classic style and would work well for her purposes. There was still a morning chill in the air, but she knew it was supposed to warm up later and she wouldn't need to bother with a coat. She clipped her hair back and put on some blush, mascara and lip gloss. She put the MacBook in its case, grabbed her cell phone, threw both of them into her bag, and went back out through the garage entrance where she saw Cord pacing alongside his car with a phone to his ear.

Cord held up his index finger indicating he would be just a minute, while at the same time walking around his car and opening the passenger door. Ellie situated herself inside and watched as Cord walked back in front of the car and got into the driver's seat, ending his call as he did so.

Glancing over at Ellie as he buckled his seat belt, Cord could sense the change in her demeanor. Gone was any sign of fear or uncertainty. He was searching for a word to describe her.

"What?" questioned Ellie as she met his appraisal.

"Nothing," said Cord. "I was just trying to decide how to sum up the way you look. Formidable. That's it. Formidable. I'm thinking I wouldn't want to be on the witness stand with you as the prosecutor."

Ellie gave a little chuckle, "Thanks, I think?"

"Oh, yeah, it looks good on you. Buckle up. We'll make a quick stop by my condo so that I can change and then we'll head into the office. Everything is set up."

They drove out the gate and Cord waved at a car that was parked a few doors down from the Nelson's house. The agent assigned to monitor the house had obviously arrived.

Cord told her his condo was located in the Crossroads district. Like many cities, downtown Kansas City and some of the adjacent areas were being revitalized. The Crossroads was one such area in lower downtown that had seen a proliferation of restaurants, art galleries, and entertainment venues that made it the new "in" place to be.

As they approached a group of buildings, Cord pointed and said, "We'll go around the corner to the alley and into the parking garage, but that's my building."

"Hotel Monroe?" Ellie questioned. "You live in a hotel?"

Cord was grinning from ear to ear and he enthusiastically explained about the building as he pulled around the block and into the parking garage. "It used to be a hotel. It was converted to condos a few years back and I was lucky that a unit was available when I was looking. I really like the condo, but it was the history of the building that sold me. It used to be owned by Thomas Pendergast back in the 20's. Pendergast contracted the same guy that designed the hotel to construct the building that sits right next to it. He used the adjacent building as the headquarters for his Jackson County Democratic Club. The cool thing was that he had a doorway installed between his second-floor office and the hotel, giving him a secret entry point and access to the hotel's elevator. There's no evidence of the entry now but it is still a great piece of history."

Cord's enthusiasm for his story was catching and both he and Ellie were still smiling as they exited the car and rode the elevator up the couple of floors to his condo. The smiles were quickly replaced with expressions of surprise as Cord opened the door and ushered Ellie in before him.

Ellie took in the sleek, modern furnishings of the room before her. But the most stunning thing in the room was the statuesque blonde that stood facing the door. Dressed in a cream colored, silk blouse and camel hair slacks, with perfect hair and make-up, she exuded an elegance and sophistication that practically screamed "old money." The smile that had been on the woman's face as the door opened, now turned into a scowl.

From behind her, Ellie heard Cord say, "Charlotte, what are you doing here?"

"Uh oh," thought Ellie, "Wrong thing to say."

There was an uncomfortable silence as Charlotte gave Cord a look that Ellie could swear had added a chill to the room.

Ellie stepped toward Charlotte and extended her hand. "Hello, I'm Ellie Nelson, you must be Cord's fiancée. You're just as beautiful as he described you. Cord, I can wait for you down in the building lobby."

Charlotte shook Ellie's hand, and while decidedly ignoring Cord, she immediately took control of the situation. There was no doubt that she felt very comfortable in Cord's home as the hostess in her came to the forefront.

"Nonsense, I wanted to surprise Cord and I've obviously accomplished that. Why don't you have a seat over at the kitchen island. I was just going to make some coffee. Would you like to join me while you're waiting for Cord to do whatever it was he was going to do?"

"That would be very nice," Ellie replied.

Cord had been standing almost dumbstruck watching the exchange between Ellie and Charlotte. He finally snapped out of it, stepped over to Charlotte and gave her a kiss on the cheek.

"It's great to see you, Charlotte. You really did surprise me and I'm sorry I can't stay and talk right now. I can explain everything later but I need to get changed and take Ellie to meet with my task force."

Cord practically fled the room, leaving Ellie with Charlotte, who still had a smile on her face, even if it did look more than a touch forced.

"How do you take your coffee?" Charlotte asked as she walked from the living area into the kitchen.

"Black will be fine."

Ellie sat at the island as she had been instructed. As she watched Charlotte, she was struck once again at how comfortable Charlotte was in Cord's home. She had obviously spent a lot of time here. It dawned on her that Charlotte was actually making a show of that fact. She moved with precision around the kitchen to make the coffee and pull mugs from the cabinets. When the coffee was ready, Charlotte remained standing in the kitchen as she handed Ellie a mug across the island.

"So, Ellie, how long have you known Cord?"

"Said the spider to the fly," thought Ellie. She didn't want to admit that she was jealous of the woman before her. And she didn't really have any reason to dislike her. After all, she had just met her. But the fact was, she didn't like Charlotte one bit. So, she smiled sweetly at Charlotte.

"Oh, goodness, I've known Cubby forever!"

"Cubby?" Charlotte sputtered.

Right then Cord came back in the room. His face had turned a bright red.

"She calls you Cubby?" Charlotte asked glaring at Cord, her voice raised and sounding about an octave higher to Ellie's ear.

"Not now, Charlotte!" Cord said in a tone somewhere between anger and exasperation. "I'm sorry, I really do need to go. We'll talk later, I promise. Come on, Ellie."

Ellie stood and followed Cord to the door. As he opened it, she turned back and said brightly, "Nice to meet you, Charlotte. Sorry to leave you with the dishes!"

As the door shut behind them, Cord grabbed Ellie's arm. "What was that about?"

"What was what about?" Ellie responded innocently. "Charlotte was just wondering how long we'd known each other. She seemed a little upset and I just thought maybe it would help if she knew we were old friends. The Cubby just kind of slipped out. Sorry."

"Oh, brother! I really didn't need this right now. Just forget it."

Ellie smiled to herself but kept quiet as they got into Cord's car and drove to the F.B.I. building. They pulled in front of a set of iron gates and a man came out of the security building set off to the side, opened the back door of the car and jumped into the back seat.

"Got her all set," he announced and then thrust his hand between the bucket seats, holding out a lanyard with a bright orange card inserted into it.

"I'm Special Agent Josh Thompson, Ma'am. Please make sure you have this with you and that it is visible at all times while you are in the building."

Ellie looked at the bright orange card inserted into a plastic sleeve hanging from the lanyard. It read VISITOR in bold black letters. In slightly smaller lettering but still quite noticeable were the words ESCORT REQUIRED AT ALL TIMES. It certainly set her apart from the agents. As Ellie slipped the lanyard around her neck, Cord was holding a key card up to a security box. They waited as the gates slid open and a heavy metal grate lowered into the ground.

"Imposing," Ellie said as Cord drove through the gate and over the now flattened barrier.

"Oh, it's usually wide open," Special Agent Thompson said. "But as soon as I mentioned who I needed the creds for, the guard raised the grate and closed the gate really quick."

Even with his dry delivery, Ellie could tell that Special Agent Thompson was a real character. She decided to play along.

"Oh, my," Ellie drawled in her best southern belle imitation, "Do they still have that unfortunate incident with a stiletto heel in my file. I have on sensible shoes today so you needn't worry."

"I like her," Thompson said to Cord as they drove into a parking area under the building. Cord had remained silent during the exchange between Thompson and Ellie. But Ellie could tell Cord was trying not to smile as the three of them exited the car and walked to an elevator where Cord inserted his key card. He punched a button and the elevator rose to the second floor.

When the elevator stopped, they exited into a small area where a guard sat behind a desk. The guard looked up.

"Good morning, Fred. She's with us," Cord said. The guard smiled, gave a thumbs-up and went back to looking at the laptop in front of him. They walked down a long hallway and finally reached a door where Cord once again held up a key card to a security pad. A green light flashed and Cord opened the door into a large room where several people could be seen working. Ten desks were situated facing each other in two rows in the center of the room. A door and two offices flanked both sides of the area and a large conference room ran the full width of the space along the back of the room. The walls separating the central area from the offices and conference room were made of glass, allowing in the sunlight from the windows along the outer building walls and keeping the area from feeling claustrophobic. In one of the offices, Ellie could see a copy machine, printer, refrigerator, microwave and most importantly for her what looked like a coffee machine.

As if he had been waiting for Ellie to finish her visual appraisal, Cord began to fill her in on the task force. "This room has been specifically designed for the type of work our task force is doing. It is self-contained, with restrooms on either side of the room and a break room that is a combination kitchenette/copy room. The task force itself consists of seven agents here in Kansas City and another seven agents in Denver with a similar setup there.

"Although I am the lead, all that really means is that I'm the one stuck with the paperwork and running interference with the S.A.C. and coordinating with my counterpart in Denver. For that, I have one of the offices. The other two offices are open for anyone's use when any privacy is needed and, of course, the conference room is used when all the bells and whistles are needed for a presentation and for virtual meetings with the Denver team. We have a standing one of those each day at 2 p.m. and any other time when one is needed. Most of the time I and the other agents like to work here in the bullpen.

"I've got some things to take care of in my office but I'll be out in the bullpen in a bit. In the meantime, Josh is going to introduce you to the rest of the team and get you situated. We're not sure how he got into the F.B.I., considering he has a sense of humor, but it might have something to do with the fact that he's the best analyst I've ever worked with."

Cord turned from Ellie and looked at Thompson. "Make sure you establish the record of evidence we discussed before you get started, Josh," he said, giving the agent a pat on the shoulder as he walked away from them toward the first office on the left.

"This way, Ma'am."

CHAPTER 23

Ellie fell in step with the agent. "Please call me, Ellie."

"Yes, M...Ellie. That'll make it easier. Please, call me Josh. The rest of the folks here are all special agents, too, but we like to drop all the formality within the team. Just too much of a mouthful."

Josh led Ellie down the gap between the desks and introduced her to three other men and two women as they made their way down to the last desk on the right. The surface was empty except for a closed laptop sitting in the center of the desk.

Josh motioned for Ellie to have a seat. Josh sat down at the desk next to her just as the woman immediately across from him stood and flung a backpack onto her shoulder.

"I'm bushed," she announced. "Tina and I just finished the last page of the file. It's up on the database. Enjoy. I've got to catch a few Z's. I'll be back for the 2 o'clock if not before."

Ellie watched as the woman who had been introduced to her as Sarah left the room. The other woman agent's name was Rachel. "Tina?" she asked, looking over at Josh.

"Tina is on the Denver team. Sarah has been working with her since last night on the translation of the shorthand pages from the hard drive that was recovered. The hard drive from your laptop at the D.A.'s office as I understand it. But let's not get ahead of ourselves. I saw you glance longingly at that coffee machine and I could use some, too. I promise it won't take long. We just need to get some things on record and I'd like to get that out of the way first."

Josh was smiling as he scooted his chair over to her desk and set a cell phone on the corner. He became serious, pressed a button on the phone and began speaking.

"Present are F.B.I. Special Agent Josh Thompson and former Denver Deputy District Attorney Eleanor

Nelson. The F.B.I. has possession of a computer hard drive that has been verified as one removed from a laptop belonging to and utilized by Miss Nelson in her capacity as Deputy District Attorney.

"Following information provided by Miss Nelson, subsequent examination of the files on the hard drive confirmed it contained pages of notes written in a form of shorthand by now deceased attorney, Robert Carter. Miss Nelson, would you describe for the record how the files came to be on your hard drive?"

Ellie hesitated only minute. She noticed the other agents had looked up from work they were doing and were listening intently as she described the chain of events.

"I was reviewing a case file in order to proceed with sentencing for a suspect who had pleaded guilty to the murder of a prominent Denver attorney. I had not been convinced of the suspect's story and was looking at a list of evidence, when one of the items jumped out at me. There was a listing for a set of keys on a silver bullet key chain.

"After I had retrieved the key chain from the police evidence locker, I discovered that I had been right in my thought the bullet might actually be a flash drive. I took the precaution of copying the information from the flash drive onto the hard drive of my laptop.

"I had briefly looked at the information copied from the flash drive. However, since the files contained scanned pages of notes written in shorthand, I made the decision to wait until I got to my office the following day to do a full translation. Before I could do that, I was terminated and both the key chain and laptop were taken from my possession prior to my being escorted from the building."

Ellie stopped speaking and leaned back in the chair.

Josh reached over and flipped open the laptop in front of Ellie.

"A copy of the files from that hard drive have been loaded to the laptop in front of you. To the best your memory, can you verify that these are the files from the laptop you had been using?"

Ellie spoke for the record, naming the folders and what they contained as she clicked on them, including the folder that held the Carter files.

"Yes, these are the files that were on my hard drive when it was confiscated from me."

"End record," Josh said into the phone. "That was great, Ellie. How about some coffee?"

After they had grabbed some coffee and returned to the bullpen, Ellie saw that Cord had come out of his office and sat at the desk immediately across from her. As she and Josh sat down, Cord addressed the team.

"Now that we have the full translation of Carter's file available to us, we want to start comparing the dates and names in his notes against the information we have gathered. The Denver team is doing the same. I've asked Ellie to join us as she has direct knowledge of the cases she prosecuted against Jack Manetti in Denver, as well as the information tying Stephen Lindsey to Robert Carter. Rachel and Todd, you concentrate on the surveillance transcripts. Peter and Gregg, you'll take the case files. Josh will work with Ellie. If you have any questions for the D.A. or K.C.P.D., give them to me and I'll get on it. I'd like to have at least a list of matches for our 2 o'clock meeting with Denver. Any details will just be icing on the cake. Anything before we get started?"

"I have something that may be related," Ellie said as she reached down and brought the MacBook out of her bag. She set it beside the laptop, opened it and began clicking on icons as she continued talking to the agents. "I had to drop a case against Jack Manetti a couple of years ago because the key witness disappeared. He is still listed as a missing person, since he hasn't turned up and there was never a body discovered. Now that I know there is a strong connection between Denver and Kansas City, I began to wonder if there were any unidentified bodies that turned up in Kansas City around the time my guy went missing. I found an article in the Star, about a John Doe pulled out of the Kaw just three days after my guy disappeared. It sounded like too much of a coincidence that the Kaw is where they found the body of the guy they think messed up the shooting down at The Lake. The article says it was the Kansas City, Kansas, police investigating the John Doe last year. So, I was wondering if it had been on your radar."

Ellie had stopped clicking and turned her MacBook around so that the screen was facing out toward the rest of the agents and they could see the Kansas City Star article she had been talking about. When she looked up, all the agents were staring at her. She wouldn't say all their jaws were dropped, but it was pretty close.

Even Cord seemed surprised, but he quickly took control. "Okay, folks, the rest of you focus on your tasks. Josh, show Ellie how to upload that article to the database and send it to me in an email as well. See if we get lucky with Carter's notes and there's something corresponding to the disappearance of that witness. In the meantime, I'll get on the phone with the Kansas City, Kansas, police department and see if we can get the files for the John Doe. Ellie, do you remember the name of the witness?"

"Yes, it was Edwin Washington. The investigating Denver Detective was Arthur Kelly. Since this laptop has a copy of my hard drive, I can get you the contact information."

"Email that information to me as well. I'll have some food brought in and we'll plan to have a working lunch in the conference room at noon. Drop any hits you get in today's meeting folder and we'll discuss them and be ready to share what we've got in our 2 o'clock with Denver."

There was an energy in the room as they all got to work going through the Carter notes. There was an occasional "yes" or "got one" indicating that one of the agents had found a match between Carter's notes and their own F.B.I. files. Sarah and Tina had done a great job translating the files, which were arranged in chronological order. It made it easy for Ellie to find the time frame her witness went missing.

"Look," she said to Josh as she pointed to a set of entries on the screen. DA wit loc to JM. Russo okays TM trip to D. Body in Kaw.

"That's gotta be it!" Josh shouted.

Ellie nodded but the words on the screen made her sad rather than excited. Josh looked over at her and saw the look on her face.

"What's wrong? This means you were right. This may be just what we need to bring the whole thing down."

"I know. I was just hoping I was wrong about one part of it. DA has to be referring to Mitchell Hanover. I just didn't want to think that he was involved. But this almost certainly indicates that he was. If he was giving information to Jack Manetti, then maybe he thought I might put two and two together and figure that out. That would make more sense for why he fired me."

"Okay, Ellie, you keep looking for anything that jumps out at you and I'll get this information added to the meeting folder and go let Cord know that it's looking likely the floater in the newspaper might be your guy. After that, we'll get someone looking to see if we can find any record of Tommy Manetti traveling back and forth between Kansas City and Denver at that time. It sure seems to me that if there was a body moved from Denver to Kansas City, Tommy might have been the guy Jack would have trusted to do it."

Ellie took a moment to go back to the first page of Carter's notes. Carter indicated that his notes were taken at weekly meetings he had with Gino Russo. It was obvious from the notes that the purpose was to document dealings between the two Manetti brothers. The implication was that Russo didn't trust the brothers and wanted to make sure they weren't undercutting him, or worse, planning to stage a sort of coup. Russo's concerns were probably valid and his death was a stroke of luck for the Manetti brothers who would no longer have to worry about that roadblock.

Although Ellie continued to look through the files, nothing else jumped out at her. There were definitely a lot of notes that showed dealings between the Manetti's but none of them rang a bell with her. She wasn't really surprised. The notes had more of a Kansas City flavor, which you would expect since they were from conversations between Carter and Russo. There were a couple of entries that Ellie thought would most likely be of interest to a Kansas City prosecutor as they seemed to be about case evidence. But most of the notes looked more like activities that had probably not come to trial. They had to do with shipments between Denver and Kansas City and it was those entries Ellie suspected caused the periodic shouts from the F.B.I. agents in the room. Although the shorthand was somewhat cryptic at times, it was pretty clear drugs as well as other merchandise were moving across states, not to mention a dead body.

The smell of pizza caused everyone in the room to look up. Cord came out of his office and quickly stepped over to Sarah who had just come through the door balancing a shoulder bag and a stack of pizza boxes. Cord took the boxes from Sarah and began walking toward the conference room.

"Lunch, everyone. Bring your laptops. Let's see what we've got and get it queued up for our meeting with Denver."

The words had barely started coming out of Cord's mouth before the agents stood and headed for the conference room. The rumbling in Ellie's stomach had her following suit. There was a general disorder as the agents positioned themselves and their equipment around the table. A couple of the agents went out and came back in with some paper plates, napkins and an assortment of sodas they had gotten from the break room.

"First, thanks to Sarah for picking up the pizza on her way back in. She called me earlier and said she couldn't let us have all the fun. After doing the translations, she couldn't sleep, knowing we were going to see several items that tied to our investigations. And she was right."

The other agents smiled and gave Sarah a thumbs-up. No one said anything because their mouths were already full of pizza.

"I was going to say dig in, but I see you all are way ahead of me. Just save me a couple of slices of that pepperoni."

With that, Cord pointed the remote control he held in his hand toward the big screen at the head of the room. He began opening up folders and moving icons of images and documents onto the screen. Ellie thought it looked like an episode from NCIS. Cord tapped on one of the icons and a photo of a man Ellie recognized filled part of the screen.

"This is a picture of Edwin Washington, the missing janitor from Ellie's case in Denver. I've been on the phone with the Kansas City, Kansas, and Denver police. As we already know, Mr. Washington did not have any prints on file, but we have confirmation that the physical characteristics are a match. Denver has taken the lead on this one and is working with the Washington family to get his dental records released. We'll get an update from them at our 2 o'clock."

Cord pointed to a folder as he spoke to one of the agents. "Gregg, the S.A.C. made a request to the K.C.P.D. for the files relating to the investigation into Robert Carter's suicide. We received those this morning. With the similarities to the way Carter's friend, Stephen Lindsey was killed, I want you to take another look at it and see if we can find anything from our surveillance or our informant that points to something the police might have overlooked at the time. I think we're all pretty much convinced, this was a murder rather than a suicide. I'd like to prove that."

Handing the remote to the agent nearest him, Cord took a seat.

"Let's go around the table and hear what the rest of you have. Slide that box of pepperoni down here."

Ellie watched and listened as each of the agents pulled up various information on the screen and described how it related to something in Carter's notes. It was all a little bitter sweet for Ellie at this point. She knew she had been the one to find the key to all this but it was all out of her hands now. Wherever the F.B.I. took the information from here, she wouldn't be a part of it. It hit her once again that she didn't have a job and wouldn't be the one to see Jack Manetti brought to justice. She sighed and rose from the table. She didn't know about anyone else but she needed a cup of coffee.

Everyone was looking at the screen and no one noticed Ellie when she slipped quietly from the room. As she walked toward the break room, the door at the front of the room opened and a man entered. He strode across the room like he owned it. And when he introduced himself, Ellie supposed that was pretty much true...or close enough.

"Special Agent in Charge, Walter Dunlap," the man said as he held out his hand to Ellie. "You must be Eleanor Nelson. I understand we have you to thank for uncovering new information for our task force."

Ellie shook the offered hand. "Please call me, Ellie. I was just doing my job, or at least what used to be my job. I have to say that watching your agents this morning makes me very confident they are going to be able to build a strong case against both Jack and Tommy Manetti. It can't happen soon enough for me."

Their conversation was interrupted when all the agents began pouring out of the conference room, heading either for the restrooms or the break room. A quick glance at her watch showed that it was about five minutes before their meeting with Denver was scheduled to begin.

Cord walked to where Ellie and the S.A.C. were standing. "I see you've met Miss Nelson. We're about to begin our meeting with Denver. Are you sitting in?"

"Yes, I talked with Cliff just a few minutes ago. Sounds like things are moving just as fast on his end as they are on ours and we decided it might help if we both attended today. That way, we can cut through some of the red tape and approve whatever actions are needed to keep this moving."

Ellie made a quick detour to the break room to grab the coffee she had originally started out for and then walked back into the conference room where she took a seat as far toward the back of the room as she could.

As soon as everyone was settled around the table, Cord picked up the remote control and pointed to the screen. An image of the conference room and the people in it filled the screen but was quickly reduced by half when an image of the conference room in Denver appeared on the other half. Cord immediately began speaking.

"Good afternoon. We have the usual team members with us here in Kansas City along with our S.A.C. Walter Dunlap and former Denver District Attorney Eleanor Nelson, whom I believe some of you know. Mike, you want to start off today?"

As Cord had mentioned, Ellie recognized several of the faces in the room in Denver, including those of Special Agent Mike Cummings and the Denver S.A.C. Clifford Jacobson. She'd had interactions with both men over the years in conjunction with various cases she had prosecuted.

"Good afternoon to everyone there as well. We have our usual task force folks present and our S.A.C.

is also joining us today. It's good to see you Miss Nelson. I speak for everyone in the room when I say we think you got a raw deal at the D.A.'s office and we're going to get you some payback based on the information you uncovered. Well done!"

The agent paused and Ellie's face turned a bright shade of red as all heads turned toward her smiling. There were some thumbs-up, a smattering of claps and a "whoot" or two heard throughout both rooms. Ellie gave an embarrassed grin and tried to shrug off the attention with a brief wave of her hand. Agent Cummings thankfully saved her from having to say anything, when he once again addressed everyone.

"Okay, we've got a lot to cover. So, let's get started. First, Edwin Washington's dental records were sent to the Kansas City, Kansas, medical examiner and we have confirmation that their John Doe was Edwin Washington. The S.A.C. personally called Hanover with that information and advised him it would be in his best interest to come in voluntarily for an interview. He also strongly advised Hanover that it would be in his best interest not to pass on the information from their call or his upcoming interview to anyone else, like Jack Manetti, for example. Hanover got the message loud and clear and is coming in for an interview late this afternoon."

For the next two hours, Ellie listened as the Denver and Kansas City agents walked through the details of the correlations between their investigations and the activities noted in Robert Carter's notes. It was their plan to do a sweep first thing Monday morning to bring in the known members of both Manetti operations on racketeering charges, as well as conspiracy to commit murder. They were confident that Carter's notes and the added threat of being an accomplice to murder would give them the leverage needed to convince some of the people in the Manetti organization to testify against Jack and Tommy.

Depending on what they learned from Denver D.A. Mitchell Hanover, the S.A.C. implied Hanover would either be encouraged to take a vacation to be far away from Monday's actions or he would be held over for charges. In Denver, Jack Manetti and his brother-in-law Zach Lando and five other known associates were going to be brought in. In Kansas City, the names included Tommy Manetti, Joey Capra, and Ashley Wilson, along with seven others. Ellie hoped that her impression of Ashley had been correct and that her only crime was one of naivety and a poor choice in men.

The meeting wrapped up with agents taking various assignments to firm up the details for their arrest warrants and to make the necessary arrangements for the teams to execute them. Cliff Jacobson and Mike Cummings were going to handle the interview with Mitchell Hanover, and although it was unspoken, it was a given that the agents would all be working the weekend to make sure everything was in place for Monday. Ellie found herself the topic of conversation once again as the meeting ended. It was generally agreed that agents would still keep watch at the Nelson house through the weekend. But once they made the sweep on Monday, it was felt Ellie would no longer be in danger and the security would no longer be needed. It was possible they would need her testimony in the future, but that would depend on how the case developed.

As the meeting broke up, Ellie stayed seated as all but one of the agents left the room, eager to get started on their particular assignments. Ellie stood as Cord walked toward her. His eyes had a sadness to them and Ellie gave him a half smile.

"This has been some day, huh?" she said.

By P. L. Gertner

"Ellie, about this morning. About, Charlotte..."

"Don't worry about this morning. You have more than enough on your plate."

"Look, Ellie, I really would like to talk. But, you're right. I can't do that right now. Things will be moving fast the next few days and will keep me and the task force busy for quite some time. On top of that, I have to go see why Charlotte chose now for a surprise visit. And, I'm sorry, that means I'm going to have to ask one of the other agents to see you home safely."

Ellie tried to keep a smile on her face and not show the disappointment she felt. "Oh, that's not necessary. I'll just call Uber."

With a bit of exasperation and frustration evident in his voice Cord immediately put a stop to that suggestion. "Not a chance. You heard what was just said. You're still in danger. I've asked Agent Alvarez to escort you home." Cord's voice softened a bit as he added, "Please don't take any chances. And after this is all over, we do need to talk."

With that, Cord motioned Ellie out of the conference room. When they reached the bullpen area, Ellie grabbed her bag and began walking toward Agent Alvarez who was waiting beside the door at the front of the room. As he reached to open the door, Ellie turned and shouted out her good-bye to the team. "Thanks, everyone. Go get 'em!"

CHAPTER 24

After dinner that night, Ellie had filled her parents in on everything that had happened and what was planned for the following week. They were glad of the prospect that everything would soon be back to normal for them. Ellie was saved from answering a question from her mother about her plans for looking for a job, when her phone rang. The Caller ID read, Clifford Jacobson.

Ellie had always liked the Denver S.A.C. and thought he was a straight-shooter. He confirmed that assessment when he told her the reason for his call.

"It's not exactly what I'd call within procedures, but I thought you deserved to hear what Mitchell

Hanover had to say when we interviewed him. Not surprisingly, Jack Manetti was investing heavily in Hanover's plan to run for Governor. In return, Hanover was supposed to feed Manetti information. Hanover was insistent that he only gave Manetti information that he thought was not crucial to a case. He found out with Edwin Washington's disappearance that he was wrong. Even though he had given out Washington's location, he knew that he was under protection and didn't think Manetti would be able to do anything about it. When Washington actually disappeared, he knew he had dug himself into a hole. He saw you as a threat because you were so tenacious. By the time the Stephen Lindsey case came along and you wouldn't drop it, he was starting to panic. He'd passed along to Manetti that you thought you had found some new evidence and Manetti had pressured him to make sure it went away. Hanover's solution was to order you to drop the case and then fire you when you didn't. He insists he didn't know the key chain was a flash drive, didn't know that the drive had been stolen in a home burglary, and had no intent to destroy evidence when he confiscated your laptop.

He also insists that he had no idea Manetti had gone after you.

"Hanover is smart enough to know that we'd have trouble prosecuting him for his involvement with either the Lindsey or Washington murders and those are the cases where we have the most evidence. However, he is also smart enough to know that the publicity would ruin his chance to run for Governor. It could also result in his disbarment. I suspect that he will eventually announce his retirement, but for now, he and his wife are going to take a spontaneous vacation. They'll be leaving tomorrow for a 21-day cruise to Australia. We're confident we will have his full cooperation when we take the Manetti's to trial."

"I really appreciate you calling me. Mitchell Hanover and I never got along but I would not have predicted any of this."

"It has been my observation over the years you were in Denver that you were one heck of a prosecutor, Ellie Nelson, and a damn fine investigator, too. If you ever want a job with the F.B.I., give me a call."

"Thanks, for the offer, but I have other plans. Good luck!"

Ellie was chuckling as she ended the call but sobered up pretty fast. She had been so wrapped up in what Jacobson was saying that she had forgotten her parents sitting across from her.

"What was that about?" asked Howard Nelson.

"What plans?" asked Evelyn Nelson.

Ellie took the easy question first and told her parents what Jacobson had said, including his offer for a job with the F.B.I. It was as good a segue as any and her mother jumped at it.

"Well, I heard you said no to that. If Hanover ends up retiring, are you considering trying to get hired back by the new D.A.?"

"Actually, Mom, I've decided I'm not going back to being a prosecutor at all?"

"What? You mean you want to go into another area of law?"

Her mother's face brightened a bit and Ellie knew what her mother would ask next. So, she saved her the trouble of asking, all the while knowing the hopeful look on her mother's face would not last as soon as she began talking about her plans.

"I know what you're thinking, Mom. I know you'd find a place for me at your firm. But, that's not what I want to do."

"Well, I have many contacts. I'm sure..."

"No, please hear me out." Ellie could feel her mother tensing up. She glanced over at her father who had a bemused expression on his face. He'd always had a sixth sense about when Ellie was about to go head to head with her mother and this was certainly going to be one of those times. He'd seldom taken sides and Ellie wondered if that would be true this time as well.

"I've decided to step away from law entirely. While I may be very good at it, I haven't been happy for some time. It has been easy to blame that on that fact that I worked for Mitchell Hanover. But when Hanover fired me, I was caught off guard, and although I might have been angry at the way he handled it, I quickly realized what I felt most was a sense of relief.

"I went to The Lake to think and did have some time to do that before everything went crazy. To make a long story short, I've got a couple of properties I want to look at down there that I think would be perfect for an art gallery."

Ellie saw the storm clouds gathering and continued on before her mother could voice any objections. "When I started the art classes earlier this year, a part of me I had all but forgotten about came alive. I no longer have the passion for practicing law; I do have a passion for art. I'm rediscovering the joy I have when I paint and I have ideas for helping others pursue their artistic talents also. That's what the gallery I want to open is all about."

There was excitement in her voice as Ellie explained her plans to her parents. The excitement faded quickly however as Ellie's mother stood up, and without saying a word, left the room. Ellie's face fell and she gave an involuntary sigh as she turned toward her father.

"Give her some time, Princess. This has been a rough week for all of us. We've both been very worried about you. I can tell you've put some thought into this. If you're sure this is what you want, let's talk tomorrow and you can give me the details. I'd like to hear your business plan. I'll see if I can calm your mother down."

With that Ellie's father patted her hand and then he, too, left the room.

Sitting there alone, Ellie realized she was exhausted. It was hard to believe that in the course of one day she had been chased by mobsters, rescued by Cord, invited to consult with the F.B.I., run into Cord's fiancée, helped to find evidence that would bring down a crime syndicate, learned that Mitchell Hanover now knew that karma was indeed a bitch, and, oh, yeah, don't forget she had completely alienated her mother.

As she dragged herself up the stairs, the one thought she desperately tried to keep out of her mind was what had not happened. She had not heard from Cord. She knew it was an irrational thought but she couldn't keep herself from wondering if Cord was busy with the Manetti investigation or if he was busy with Charlotte. She had gotten used to seeing Cord every day. She had enjoyed the times he had come over for dinner and they had all discussed what was happening. He was comfortable around her parents and that was rarely true of anyone. But she knew what she would miss most was the way she had felt when Cord wrapped her in his arms that morning. And try as she might to forget it, that was the thought that stayed with her as she finally got into bed. Mercifully, she was so exhausted she was asleep almost as soon as her head hit the pillow.

When Ellie woke the next morning, she had a renewed purpose. In the back of her mind she wondered how the F.B.I. agents, and one agent in particular, were doing preparing for their round up of the Manetti's. She had no intention of adding any distractions for the team and planned to do as Cord had asked and stay put all weekend. She had lots to do to put the plans for her art gallery in motion.

Over the weekend she took her father up on his offer to help craft her business plan. With his help she was able to turn her thoughts and ideas into a solid plan. She had some money her great-grandmother had left her and it was that money she was going to use to purchase a building and set up a gallery. Ellie thought her great-grandmother would be very pleased that the money was used for that purpose and her father agreed.

Although her mother remained somewhat cool, Ellie noticed she seemed to linger in the kitchen whenever she and her father were working together. With Thanksgiving fast approaching, she spent as much time as she could, helping her mother prepare for the guests and meal she would be hosting later that week. While she might never be fully on board, Ellie was hopeful she would be able to convince her mother that this was what was best for her.

Monday rolled around and her parents had left for work. She couldn't help but be anxious, wondering what was happening with the F.B.I. Late in the morning there was a buzz signaling someone was at the front gate. Ellie's heart skipped a beat hoping it was Cord. Although it was an agent, the voice she heard wasn't Cord's. Ellie knew there was no way she should have expected it to be Cord. He would definitely have his hands full that day. But that didn't mean she didn't *wish* that it was Cord.

Ellie opened the gate and walked to the front door. She opened the door and invited the agent in.

"I can't stay, Ma'am," he said as he stepped inside to the foyer. "I just wanted to let you know that I'm leaving. I'm supposed to tell you that although there won't be a security detail any longer, you should still take caution."

"Does that mean they have the Manettis in custody?

"I can't comment on any details, Ma'am. But I was told that, if you asked, I could tell you things had gone as planned."

With that, the agent handed her a card and said she should contact the number on the card if there were any problems. Ellie thanked the agent, and as she closed the door behind him, she gave a quick glance at the card he had left. It was a generic F.B.I. card. The message was clear. If there was trouble, it wasn't Cord's number she was supposed to call.

Ellie texted both her parents to let them know the security detail was no longer there. She refused to let herself be upset that she had not heard from Cord. She had plenty to do to keep herself busy.

She was on the phone for several hours. Ellie and her friend Lisa had agreed that Ellie would fly into Denver and Lisa would help her pack up the things she wanted to take back with her to The Lake. Whatever furniture Ellie wanted or that Lisa didn't want to keep would be put in storage until Ellie had found a place to live at The Lake. While she and her parents had agreed that Ellie would initially live at their Lake house, Ellie planned to find a place of her own.

Ellie made airplane reservations and arranged for moving and storage. Then she talked with a real estate agent about the properties at The Lake she was interested in looking at for her gallery. They made an appointment to look at the properties as soon as Ellie was back from closing out things in Denver.

EPILOGUE

Ellie was happier than she had been in a long time. She had enjoyed spending some time in Denver with her friend Lisa as they packed up her painting supplies, her clothes, and a few pictures and mementos that she wanted to take back to Missouri. Other than the dining room set Lisa said she could use, movers had come and packed up the rest of Ellie's condo and had taken them to a storage facility. The Prius had been traded in on a small 4x4 truck that Ellie knew would be much more useful for the gallery and it worked out great to carry all the stuff she wanted to take with her from Denver.

Originally, Lisa had planned to take some vacation and ride back with Ellie to keep her company. But, with Ellie having been fired and Hanover on an extended vacation, the D.A.'s office was in a bit of chaos. Lisa felt she needed to stay and Ellie knew whatever time Lisa could find to get away from the office would be needed to make her own move into Ellie's condo.

With a promise from Lisa that she would be there for the grand opening of her art gallery, Ellie had given her friend a hug and started off one morning at 0 dark 30 on what she knew was a long, monotonous drive across eastern Colorado and the entire length of Kansas. The route she had taken was almost all interstate and Ellie had made it to the Lake of the Ozarks just after dark the same day. For the most part, Ellie didn't mind being alone on the drive. It had given her time to think about what she had planned for the gallery. The only downside was that she still hadn't heard a word from Cord.

She had told herself she needed to move on. Her head was on board with that, but her heart was still having some issues. That was pretty obvious when her heart sped up just a little bit every time her phone rang. And it caused her to sigh each time the caller had not been Cord. It hadn't helped much when, about halfway through Kansas, her mother had called her. She'd said she was just checking to make sure Ellie wasn't having any problems on her drive, but the real reason for her call became clear right before she hung up.

"Oh, by the way, Eleanor, I happened to be talking to Catherine Sinclair last night and she mentioned that Cord and Charlotte had called off their engagement. Isn't that interesting? I've got to run. Send your father and me a text when you arrive safely."

That had made it difficult to keep Cord out of her thoughts. What did that mean anyway? Did it mean they had just delayed their wedding plans or had they broken up completely? That just made her head spin.

Fortunately, when she had gotten back to The Lake, she had been very busy and she hadn't had much time to think about anything else aside from the gallery. Of course, she'd been keeping up with both the Denver and Kansas City papers and knew that the Manetti brothers would be brought to trial. That made Ellie think the F.B.I. had been successful in getting one or more of the men working for the Manettis to corroborate the evidence against them.

She had no doubt those witnesses were in protective custody.

The good thing about all that was that the Manettis had much bigger things to worry about than her. She was no longer the key to what was in Robert Carter's files. The F.B.I. had those files and the Manettis would be well aware of that now. She was still mindful of her surroundings but hadn't felt even an inkling that she had been in danger.

She had met with her realtor and looked at the two buildings she thought might work for her. She had selected one on the Bagnell Dam Strip. The Strip, as it was called locally, was being revitalized and had restaurants and shops designed to draw in the tourists. From May through September, The Strip was alive with activities. She thought she would get a lot of tourist traffic for the gallery and hoped that her studio concept would be a draw with the locals year-round.

The building she had bought was two stories with windows across the front on both floors. Even the door was inset with a full-length glass panel. The light streamed into the building. It would be perfect for the gallery on the first floor and the studio she envisioned on the second floor. Even better was the fact that the zoning was flexible and there was enough space in the back of the upper floor to build out a small apartment.

Ellie had been able to close quickly on the property. She had decided on The Artist's Corner as the name for her business, but not before she had teased her parents, telling them she was going to name it The Nelson Art Gallery. It had been a family joke, or as some thought a curse, that they shared a name with the art institute in Kansas City. When being introduced to anyone, they usually had to add, "no relation to THAT Nelson."

Yes, Ellie was happy. She had just finished her second meeting with her contractor to sign the papers that would get him and his crew started the next day on construction. After closing and locking the door after the contractor, Ellie did a couple of spontaneous pirouettes across the natural hardwood floor. She heard a tap on the door and turned, thinking the contractor must have forgotten something.

She could clearly see the man standing at the glass door, looking somewhat apprehensive. It wasn't the contractor.

Ellie quickly walked over and opened the door. "Hello, Cord."

By P. L. Gertner

A Note from the Author

If you want to contact me or would like information about upcoming books, check out my website: gertnermedia.com